W9-CUY-758

Confidentially Yours

Confidentially Yours

Charles Williams

OVERLOOK DUCKWORTH
New York • London

This edition published in the United States and the United Kingdom in 2014 by
Overlook Duckworth, Peter Mayer Publishers Inc.

NEW YORK:
141 Wooster Street
New York, NY 10012
www.overlookpress.com
For bulk and special sales, please contact sales@overlookny.com,
or write us at the above address.

LONDON:
30 Calvin Street
London E1 6NW
www.ducknet.co.uk
info@duckworth-publishers.co.uk
For bulk and special sales, please contact sales@duckworth-publishers.co.uk,
or write us at the above address.

Copyright © 1962 by Charles Williams

All rights reserved. No part of this publication may be reproduced or
transmitted in any form or by any means, electronic or mechanical,
including photocopy, recording, or any information storage and
retrieval system now known or to be invented, without permission
in writing from the publisher, except by a reviewer who wishes to
quote brief passages in connection with a review written for
inclusion in a magazine, newspaper, or broadcast.

This is a work of fiction. Names, characters, places, and incidents either are
the product of the author's imagination or are used fictitiously. Any resemblance to
actual persons, living or dead, businesses, companies, events, or locales is entirely
coincidental.

Cataloging-in-Publication Data is avaliable from the Library of Congress
A catalogue record for this book is available from the British Library

Printed in the United States of America

ISBN: 978-1-4683-0855-6 US
ISBN: 978-0-7156-4911-4 UK

2   4   6   8   10   9   7   5   3   1

CHAPTER 1

THE DAY IT BEGAN WAS January 5th. I'd gone hunting that morning, and it was a little after one P.M. when I got to the office.

Clebourne's the main street, and the central business district is about seven blocks long. Warren Realty is in the second block from the west end, with J.C. Penney's on one side and Fuller's cafe on the other, and, except that it's mine, it could be any small-town real estate office anywhere—the plate glass window with a few of the current listings posted in it, a split-leaf philodendron here and there, two salesmen's desks forever cluttered with papers, and, as a sort of focal point like the medulla oblongata of the human nervous system, another desk with a typewriter, several telephones, a Notary sign, and a girl who knows where everything is buried, including the bodies. The girl in this case is Barbara Ryan, if girl is the correct term for a 30-year-old divorcee. She has reddish mahogany-colored hair that always seems a little tousled, a wide mouth in a rather slender face, cool blue eyes, and an air of good-natured cynicism, as though she were still fond of the human race in spite of the fact she no longer expected a great deal of it. When I came in she was alone in the office, speaking into one of the telephones.

"Just a moment, please. Here's Mr. Warren now." Then she added, "It's long-distance."

That was probably Frances now, calling to say she was on her way home. I'd tried twice the night before to call her, but she hadn't come back to the hotel. "Thanks," I said. "I'll take it inside." I went back to my office and closed the door, grabbing up the phone as I dropped into the chair behind the desk. "Hello."

It was Frances. "Really, John," she said petulantly, "do you have to bark? Didn't the girl tell you it was me?"

Here we go again, I thought. She should realize by this time that the only way I can speak over a telephone is abruptly; I've tried, but I can't change it. Also, she knew Barbara's name as well as I did, and I could see no reason for referring to her as "the girl." I brushed aside the annoyance. "Sorry, honey. I tried to get you last night—"

"Yes. I know. But after the concert, the Dickinsons wanted to do Bourbon Street, so it was after three when I got back to the hotel, and it was too late to call back then. I just woke up; in fact, I'm still lying here in bed."

I thought of the way she looked lying in bed, the swirl of dark hair across the pillow, the blue-green eyes in the beautifully made and sensuous face, the long smooth legs, and began to feel more than ever like an underprivileged husband. "What time are you starting back? Are you all packed?"

"No-o, dear. That's one reason I called; I'm thinking of staying over till Sunday."

"*What?*"

"The Dickinsons have invited me to dinner tonight. And tomorrow there's a cocktail party—"

"But, dammit, honey, you've been gone a week now."

"Well, really, John, it's just two more days. And you'll probably be duck-hunting anyway."

"No. I was out this morning—" I stopped; there was no use arguing about it. Even if I got her to change her mind, it wouldn't be any good. She'd arrive in a bad mood and there'd be an argument, or several days of sweet martyrdom, which was worse. Maybe I was being selfish, anyway. "Okay, honey. But make it Sunday, will you?"

"Of course, darling." There was a slight pause, and then she added, "Oh, by the way, I'll probably have to cash a check today."

"Sure," I said. "How much?"

"Do I hear five hundred?" she asked playfully. "I have to do some shopping, and that's a nice round number."

"Good God!"

"Was that another bark, dear, or more in the nature of a growl?"

"It was a grunt," I said. "I was getting up off the floor. Look, honey, you've got every credit card known to man, and charge accounts at most of the stores down there." I was about to add that she'd also had six hundred in cash when she left here, but thought better of it and didn't.

"But I don't have any account at this shop, dear," she explained patiently, "and they have the most adorable suit, and the accessories. It's a Balenciaga copy, and I think I have the figure for it."

She knew damned well she did. "As I seem to remember it," I said, "you do, though it's been some time since I've been able to check. Okay, sexy, but when you get it dressed, will you for God's sake bring it home?"

She laughed. "I love it when you sound like Boyer."

There was something in the background that sounded like a trumpet. "Don't tell me you've bought an orchestra," I said.

"It's the radio," she replied. "I'll turn it off. But never mind, I'd better start dressing. I'll see you Sunday, dear."

After she'd hung up, I was still conscious of vague dissatisfaction. Maybe it was the day; it was still and oppressive, with that feeling of uneasiness that precedes a storm. We'd successfully skirted an argument, but I wondered if I'd backed down too easily. Some friends of hers in New Orleans had had an extra ticket to the Sugar Bowl game; I hadn't been able to get away, even if another ticket had been obtainable, so she'd gone alone. The original three-day trip had stretched to a week, and now it was nine days. I didn't like it, but there didn't seem to be a great deal I could do about it. I thought wryly of the surprise this pussyfooting attitude would cause among a large part of Carthage's population who considered me an outspoken hothead who was always charging headlong into something with at least one foot in his mouth.

We'd been married less than two years. Was it the town she was bored with, or me? She'd grown up in Florida, mostly in Miami. Carthage, God knows, is no hectic round of gaiety, but at the moment I wasn't too sure it was the town. I tried to take an objective look at this fellow who called himself John Duquesne Warren, but I suppose it's impossible; the picture is always clouded by the mood. Sometimes I was able to see myself as quite a lad—sharp, aggressive, successful, popular—but all that came through now was yesterday's second-string tackle with a receding hairline, the small-town businessman with a fading and beat-up dream or two, a beautiful but sometimes puzzling wife, no children, and a few jokes his friends were probably heartily sick of hearing—a nonentity and a crashing bore. Nobody would ever name a bridge after me, or a disease, or a gazelle.

Except for eight years away at school and one in Korea, I'd lived here all my life. My mother, who died when I was eight, had left me three pieces of commercial property on Clebourne Street, one of which I'd sold, using the proceeds to speculate in Florida real estate. I'd made a fair minor-league fortune out of it. I still owned the other two properties, which brought in a comfortable income. Warren Realty was in one, and the other was the old Duquesne Building on the northeast corner of Clebourne and Montrose, which contained Lackner Optical, the Sport Shop, and Allen's Stationery store, as well as the professional offices on the second floor. My father, who was in the Citizens National Bank, had died in 1952, while I was in Korea.

It was right here in the office that I'd first met Frances. She came in one morning, two years ago this week, and wanted to rent the vacant store space in the Duquesne Building—the one now occupied by the Sport Shop, with the living quarters in back—to open a dress shop. My first impression was that no woman that good-looking and that young—she was only 25—could know anything about running a business, but develop it she did. She and her husband had owned a very successful dress shop in Miami until they'd split up the year before. After the divorce she'd wanted to get away from Miami and had started for the Coast in her car, stopped overnight in Carthage, and became interested in its possibilities. In the end I rented her the space, and then in less than six months did myself out of a tenant by persuading her to marry me...

I tried to shrug off this mood of futility, and attacked the accumulation of paperwork on my desk. Evans, one of the salesmen, came in to discuss an offer he'd received on one of the listings. At three I went next door to Fuller's for a cup of coffee. The cold front was going to be on us in less than an hour; angry masses of clouds, dark and swollen with turbulence, were beginning to pile up in the northwest. People were rolling up the windows of parked cars and keeping an eye on it as they hurried along the sidewalks. I wished it had come through before daybreak this morning, as originally forecast; I might have got some ducks.

Barbara came in to take some letters. She was sitting in the chair near the corner of the desk with her legs crossed, the shorthand notebook on her thigh, and as I dictated I found my train of thought being interrupted from time to time. It would be asinine to say she had worked for me for over a year without my ever having noticed that she was a very attractive girl, but this was apparently the first time I'd ever consciously thought of it. Leaning forward as she was, a strand of reddish-brown hair had swung down alongside her face, framing the line of her cheek. She was wearing a blouse with long full sleeves gathered closely at the wrists, and I found my eyes returning time after time to the slender, fine-boned hands below them with their delicate tracery of blue veins and the tapering fingers moving so gracefully at their work. I stumbled in mid-sentence.

Without looking up she read back, "—not presently included within the corporate limits of the city of Carthage comma nor expected to be so included within—" One corner of her mouth twitched humorously. "Not 'foreseeable future', I hope?"

I grinned. "No. I've often wondered what that meant, myself. How about 'near future'?"

I went on, but I was still having difficulty concentrating on the letter. I was disgusted with myself and wondered if that was what I was going to become, a middle-aged ogler of secretaries. It wasn't difficult to imagine the contempt she'd feel if she were aware of this scrutiny; she'd already had one experience with a philandering husband—her own. Just then, before I could stumble again, the telephone rang. She answered it, and passed it to me. "It's the Sheriff."

"Sheriff?" I repeated stupidly, wondering what Scanlon would be calling here for. "Hello."

"Warren? Listen, did you go hunting this morning? Out at Crossman Slough?"

"Yes," I said. "Why?"

"What time?"

"I got there a little before daylight, and left—I think it was about a quarter of ten."

"You didn't see anything of Dan Roberts out there?"

I frowned. "No. I saw his car, though. What's this all about?"

"He killed himself. I'm trying to get some idea of what time."

"*Killed himself?*"

"Yes. Dr. Martin and Jimmie MacBride found him about a half hour ago, and called in from Vernon's store. Doc said he'd blown most of the side of his head off, and apparently it happened sometime early this morning. He was in that blind around to the right from the end of the road, the number two, I think you fellows call it. Where were you?"

"Number one. Straight down from the end of the road. But, good God, how'd he do it?"

"I don't know. Mulholland's out there now, with the ambulance. Doc said the gun must have been practically in his face when it went off, so I guess he was picking it up by the barrel. Was he still doing any shooting over there when you left?"

"No," I said. "There was nothing to shoot at. I never saw a duck the whole morning. The only shots I heard were just about daybreak."

"That would have been before legal opening hour."

"I know," I said. "I remember being a little burned about it and wondering who it was. We're pretty strict about that."

"It'd have to be Roberts, because you two were the only ones out there. I've talked to everybody else. But did you say *shots*?"

"That's right. Two."

"How close together?"

I thought about it. "It's hard to say, but probably less than a minute apart."

"Not like a man trying for a double on a flight of ducks?"

"No. Too far apart for that. They'd have been out of range before he got off the second one. It was more as if he'd knocked down a cripple that started to get up so he had to shoot it again. That's what I thought it was, actually. A single."

"Nothing came over you?"

"No. As I said, I didn't see a duck the whole morning. The chances are they would have flared out over that number one blind where I was, because it's on that point between the two arms of the slough, and even if they'd gone behind me I'd have heard the wings."

"It's damn funny, all right. And you never heard anything at all after that?"

"Not a sound."

"I see. Oh, there's one more thing. You don't know anything about his next of kin?"

"No," I said. "I'm sorry. My understanding is he came from Texas, but I'm not sure where."

"Well, we'll try the store, and his personal gear. Thanks."

Barbara was watching wide-eyed as I hung up. I told her about it. "Oh, no!" she exclaimed. "How awful."

"It's a rotten shame." He was probably still in his twenties. But at least he didn't have a wife and children to break the news to, as far as I knew. In spite of the fact he was a tenant of mine, I didn't know a great deal about him other than the fact he was a deadly shot at skeet and drove a high-powered sports car. He was a lean, dark, Indian-looking type who was pleasant enough but never talked much about himself. He'd come to Carthage about ten months ago and opened the Sports Shop in the Duquesne Building, in the same space where Frances had had her dress shop, and lived in the small apartment behind it. Just before hunting season he'd joined the Duck Club, buying Art Russell's membership when Art moved to Florida. We kept it limited to eight members.

But how had he done it? While I'd never hunted with him, I had shot skeet with him a couple of times at the Rutherford Trap and Skeet Club, and he was a natural with a gun. He followed the safety rules in that automatic way of men who've been handling guns all their lives. But then hunting accidents were nearly always inexplicable. I tried to push it out of my mind and go on with the letters, but the feeling of depression persisted.

The storm struck a few minutes after five. I went out front and stared through the window at the rain-lashed street where the ropes of tinsel still up from Christmas whipped and billowed in the wind. Evans and Turner had already gone. Barbara was covering the typewriter and taking her purse from a drawer.

"I'll run you home," I said.

She smiled, but shook her head. "Thanks. I brought my car today."

Just as she was going out the door the telephone rang. I motioned for her to go ahead, and picked it up myself. It was

Scanlon again. "Warren? Can you get over to the courthouse right away?"

"Sure," I said. "What is it?"

"It's about Roberts."

"Have you been able to figure out how it happened?"

"We're not sure. I'll tell you about it when you get here."

I locked the front door and made a run for the car. It was only three blocks over to the. courthouse on Stanley, the second street north of Clebourne. It was perceptibly colder now, and already growing dark under the downpour. I found a parking place near the entrance and dashed up the steps.

The sheriff's office was on the lower floor left. It was a big room, separated from the doorway by a chest-high counter and a railing with a gate. On the far wall was a large-scale map of the county and a glass-fronted case containing several .30-30 carbines and a couple of tear-gas guns, while most of the space on the right was taken up by a battery of filing cabinets. There were four desks with green-shaded droplights above them. Mulholland, the chief deputy, was standing at the end of one of the desks near the left side of the room, intent on several objects atop it under the hot cone of light. One was a Browning double-barreled shotgun with the breech open, while the others appeared to be a shotgun shell, an envelope, and some photographs. Just as I approached, Scanlon emerged from his private office at the left beyond the desk. He was a big man, still slender and flat-bellied in middle age, and was coatless, the collar of his shirt unbuttoned and the tie pulled open. The graying hair was rumpled and he looked tired, but the hawk-beaked face and gray eyes were expressionless.

Without a word he handed me one of the big 8-by-10 photographs. I looked at it and felt my stomach start to come up into my throat. It had apparently been taken in the entrance to the duck blind. Roberts had fallen back into the small boat in which he'd been sitting, most of the side of his head blown away above the right eyebrow and the eye itself exploded out of the socket by some freak of hydrostatic pressure. I shuddered and put it down on the table, and when I looked up Scanlon's eyes were on my face.

"Did you shoot him?" he asked.

I was still shaken, and it didn't penetrate at first. "What?"

"I said, did you shoot him?"

"Are you crazy? Of course I didn't—"

He cut me off. "Look, Warren, better men than you have shot someone accidentally, and panicked. If you did, say so now, while you can."

"I've told you already," I said hotly. "I didn't even see him. And I don't appreciate—"

"Keep your hair on." He took a cigar from his shirt pocket and bit the end off it. "I just asked you."

"I thought you said he shot himself."

"That was what we were supposed to think," Mulholland put in with a supercilious smile. He was a big, flashy ex-athlete who always walked as if he were watching himself in a mirror. I'd never liked him.

"What do you mean?" I asked.

"He wasn't killed with his own gun."

"How do you know?"

He shrugged, and looked at Scanlon. "You want me to tell him?"

Scanlon was lighting his cigar. He waved a hand. "Go ahead."

Mulholland pointed to the shotgun. "Both barrels were loaded, but only one had been fired. Here's the empty shell." He touched the empty with his finger, rolled it over so the printing was uppermost. "See? Number 6 shot, it says."

"Yes. So?"

He moved his hand to the white envelope, tilted it, and six or eight shot pellets rolled out onto the surface of the desk. "So these are some of the shot we took out of his head, and they're number 4's."

CHAPTER 2

I STARED FROM ONE TO the other. "Are you sure?" I asked at last.

"Positive," Scanlon said bluntly. "We've compared them with 4's and 6's from new shells, and miked 'em—the ones that're still round—and weighed 'em at the physics lab out at the high school. These shot are number 4's. And the fired shell was loaded with 6's."

"Well, wait—maybe it was a reload. I'll admit it would be silly for him to reload his own shells when he could buy 'em wholesale."

Scanlon shook his head. "It was no reload. It was a new shell, right from the factory. The same as the unfired one in the gun, and the other 23 in his hunting coat, out of a new box of 25. Somebody killed him, and then fired his gun to make it look like an accident. That's the reason you heard two shots from over there."

"If he did," Mulholland said.

I turned and looked at him. "How was that again?"

"I said, if you did hear two shots—from that other blind."

"If you want to ask me any questions," I told Scanlon, "you'd better send your boy home, or tell him to keep his remarks to himself. We're not going to get anywhere this way."

"Shut up, both of you!" he snapped. He turned to me. "Now, you say you got out there before daylight. Was there any other car parked at the end of the road besides Roberts'?"

"There was no car at all when I got there."

"I thought you said you saw his car."

"When I was leaving," I explained. "I was already in the blind when the other car got there. I didn't know whose it was then, of course; I just saw headlights flashing through the trees. When I started home, somewhere around ten o'clock, it was still there, and I saw it was Roberts' Porsche."

"And you never did see any other car?"

"No."

"Could there have been one without your seeing it?"

"It's not likely, unless he drove in with his lights off, which would be a little hard to do on a road through heavy timber, or unless he arrived after daylight."

"But at the time you heard those two shots from the other blind it was still too dark to drive without lights?"

"Yes."

"That blind you were in is the nearest one to the end of the road. Did Roberts try to come out to it?"

"No," I said. "When he saw my car there, he'd have been pretty sure it was occupied. It's the best location of the four, and always taken on a first-come first-served basis."

"Was the gate out there at the highway locked when you went in?"

"Yes," I said. "And locked when I came out."

He nodded. "Still, Roberts could have forgotten to lock it after him when he came in, and whoever killed him could have followed him almost to the parking area before he left his car. Going out, he wouldn't need a key to close a padlock. On the other hand, of course, he could have walked in all the way. It's less than three miles from the highway."

"You mean you actually believe somebody went out there deliberately to murder him?"

Scanlon nodded, his eyes bleak. "What else is there? He went hunting alone. You were the only other person out there. He didn't shoot himself. So somebody shot him in cold blood. And then tried to set up this phony accident. He might have got away with it, too, if he'd thought to check the size shot Roberts was shooting."

"But why?" I asked blankly. "Who'd have any reason to kill him?"

"If we knew that, he'd be down here now. You can't think of anybody he's ever had trouble with?"

"No," I said.

"How did you get along with him?"

"All right. He was a good tenant, paid his rent on time, no beefs."

"You usually use number 4 shot for ducks, don't you?" Mulholland asked.

"That's right," I said. "I always do. And I was shooting 4's today. Why?"

He gave me a cold smile. "I just wanted to be sure."

"Good. Then your mind's at rest. Go put some more hair tonic on it."

Scanlon cursed us, and broke it up. We were an intelligent pair, I thought sourly, grown men acting like children. It was a legitimate question, under the circumstances, but I didn't like the dirty way he put it. He always rubbed me the wrong way.

"Weren't there any fingerprints on the gun?" I asked.

"No," Scanlon said. "Not even Roberts."

"Somebody wiped 'em off," Mulholland said. "Clever, huh?"

I ignored him this time, and spoke to Scanlon. "Is that all?"

He was staring moodily at the shotgun. "Oh? Yeah, that's all. Thanks for coming down."

I went back to the car. It was too early for dinner and I couldn't face the thought of a whole evening in that empty house, so I went back to the office and worked on a rough draft of my income tax until after eight before going into Fuller's. Everybody was talking about Roberts, and I had to repeat what I knew about it a half-dozen times. It was around ten when I drove home. The house is only six blocks from downtown, a rambling cream-colored brick I'd built when Frances and I were married, replacing the old Warren house which had burned down in 1955. An extension of the circular drive goes back along the side of it to the two-car garage, which adjoins the kitchen. The house is roughly U-shaped, with the kitchen and dining room in the short wing, the long 35-foot living room and my den across the front with the entrance hall between them while, a continuation of the hall runs back through the other wing past the guest rooms to the master bedroom with its fireplace, dressing room, and bath taking up the far end.

Rain, wind-driven, beat against the house. I mixed a drink and tried to settle down in the living room with a book, but it was no good. I kept thinking of Roberts. It was fantastic. Why would somebody have wanted to kill him? And why out there— aside from the futile attempt to make it appear an accident? Only eight of us had keys to that gate. Besides Roberts and myself, there were Dr. Martin; Jim MacBride, the Ford dealer; George Clement, the town's leading attorney; Clint Henry, cashier of the Citizens National Bank; and Bill Sorensen and Wally Albers, who were away at the moment, on a cruise to Jamaica with their wives.

They were all good friends of mine. Of course, as Scanlon said, Roberts might have left the gate open when he came in, or the man could have walked in, but even so he'd have to be familiar with the terrain and the location of the blinds to get there, three miles from the highway, in the dark. The turnoff was fifteen miles east of town.

I went out and mixed another drink. The telephone rang. There's an extension in the kitchen; I sat down at the table in. the breakfast nook and reached for it.

"Is this Duke Warren?" It was a girl's voice.

"Yes," I said. "Who's this?"

"Never mind. I just thought I'd tell you—you won't get away with it."

I frowned. "Get away with what?"

"I suppose you think because you own most of the town they won't do anything. Well, I've got news for you."

Somebody on a telephone jag, I thought, though she didn't sound drunk. "I'll tell you, why don't you call me in the morning?"

"Don't try to brush me off. You know what I'm talking about. Dan Roberts."

I'd started to hang up, but caught myself just in time when I heard the name. "Roberts?" I snapped. "What about him?"

"If you had to kill somebody, why not her? You don't think he was the only one, do you?"

I slammed the receiver down on the cradle and stood up, shaking with rage. When I tried to light a cigarette, I fumbled and dropped it in my drink. In a few minutes I began to get it under control, realizing it was childish to let a thing like that get under my skin. Nobody paid any attention to psychos and creeps. They crawled out of the woodwork every time something happened, spewed up their anonymous telephone calls, and went back.

I washed out the glass and rebuilt the drink, tried the cigarette again, and got one alight this time, regretting now that I'd hung up on her. I should have made some effort to find out who she was. The telephone rang again. I went over and picked it up, very coldly this time. But it was probably somebody else; she wouldn't have the guts to call back.

She did. "Don't hang up when I'm talking to you. You're in no position to."

"No?" I asked. "Why not?" I knew practically everybody in town; maybe if she kept talking I could identify her. The voice was vaguely familiar.

"Maybe you think Scanlon's a fool? Or afraid of you?"

She didn't sound particularly bright; nobody who'd known Scanlon as long as an hour could have any illusions as to his being a fool, or that he'd ever been afraid of anything. "Get to the point," I said. "What about Scanlon?"

"I think he'll be interested to learn that she's been going to Dan's apartment. Of course, she used to live there, so maybe she just forgets she's moved."

"You bet he'll be interested," I said. "So I'll tell you what you do. Go down to the sheriff's office right now and tell him about it. I'll meet you there, and when you get through I'll file charges against you for slander and defamation of character."

"Don't bet on it. I just might have proof."

"Well, don't forget to bring it when you come out from under your rock, because you're sure as hell going to need it."

"I'm talking about a cigarette lighter. Or didn't you know that's where she lost it?"

"I don't know why it's any of your business," I said, "but she hasn't lost it."

"Are you sure, now? A thin gold lighter with a couple of fancy initials that look like F.W.? It's a—hmmm—Dunhill. Sweet dreams, Mr. Warren." This time she hung up.

I sat there for a moment, feeling vaguely uneasy; that was Frances' lighter she'd described. And now that I thought of it, she *had* said something about it, two or three weeks ago. Then I remembered. It had needed repairs, a new spark wheel or something, so she'd sent it back to the store in New York where I'd bought it for her. As a matter of fact, it was probably here now. I jumped up and went out to the living room; unless I was mistaken, a small parcel had come for her since she'd been in New Orleans. I yanked open the drawer of the table where I'd put her mail, and was conscious of relief and, at the same time, a faint twinge of guilt that I'd even felt it necessary to check. It was a small, flat package, insured parcel post, and it was from Dunhill's in New York.

As I dropped it back in the drawer, I noticed the letter under it was from her brokerage firm in New Orleans, and wondered idly if she'd been switching stocks without asking my advice. Not that it mattered particularly; it was only a small account, around six thousand dollars, and hers personally, the money she'd received from the stock and fixtures of the dress shop when we were married.

I sat down with my drink, still trying to clean the telephone call out of my mind. Who was the girl, and what was her object in a thing like that? Some nut with a grudge against the whole human race, or did she have some specific reason to hate Frances, or me? She must have known Roberts pretty well; once she'd referred to him by his first name. The voice had been tantalizingly familiar, but I still couldn't place her. And how had she described the lighter so well? Of course, she could have seen Frances using it somewhere, but why the odd phrasing? *It's a—hmmm—Dunhill.* If that was deliberate, it was damned clever; it gave the impression she was holding it in her hand as she spoke.

She *wasn't* that clever, I thought, beginning to feel a chill between my shoulder blades. Cursing, I strode back to the table, and yanked open the drawer again. Tearing off the wrappings, I flipped up the lid of the velvet-covered box. It was the same gold-plated lighter, with the same ornate monogram, but it was a brand-new one.

For what must have been a full minute I stood looking stupidly down at it, and then around the room, trying to reorient myself the way you do after being hit hard at football. There must be some mistake. Maybe they'd given her this one to replace the old one, on a guarantee, or something. No, the receipted sales slip was under it, with a refund voucher for overpayment. She'd sent a check. I turned and grabbed the telephone, and it wasn't until the long-distance operator was putting through the call that I wondered what I was going to say to her. This had to be done face to face. Well, I could tell her to come home. The hotel switchboard answered.

"Mrs. Warren, please," I said.

"I believe she's checked out," the girl replied. "One moment, please; I'll give you the desk."

She'd said she was going to stay over till Sunday. What had changed her mind so suddenly? "Desk," a man's voice said.

"This is John Warren. I'm trying to reach my wife on a very urgent matter. Could you tell me how long ago she checked out?"

"Yes, sir. It was shortly before seven this evening."

"Do you know whether she received a long-distance call? Or made one?"

"Hmmm—I think there was a call for her from Carthage, Alabama, but she didn't get it—"

"How's that?" I interrupted.

"It was before she came in. Around five-thirty."

"Was there any message, or a number to call back?"

"No, sir. There was no information at all, so we didn't make out a slip on it. I just happened to remember it because Mrs. Warren asked when she came in if there'd been any calls, and I checked with the board and told her about it. She made no calls herself, though; we have no toll charges on the bill."

"Wait—you mean besides the one at one-thirty this afternoon?"

"No. There were none at all, Mr. Warren."

I was gripping the receiver so hard my fingers hurt, and I had to restrain an impulse to shout. "You'd better check again if your information's no better than that. She called me at one-thirty."

"It must have been from outside the hotel, sir. We always clear with the switchboard when making up the bill, especially on unscheduled checkouts, and we have no record of it."

I'm still lying here in bed... Well, she hadn't said whose. I traced a thoughtful doodle along the table top with my forefinger, said, "Thank you very much," and dropped the receiver back on the cradle. As I was turning away I suddenly remembered the three or four trumpet notes I'd heard in the background when she was talking to me, and it struck me now there'd been something oddly familiar about them. God, had she been on a military reservation? No—I'd spent a good part of my life being ordered by buglers in the Army and in military schools when I was a boy, and even with my tin ear I could recognize any of the calls after the first few notes. It was something else. It must have been just music, which to me was always a more or less unintelligible jumble of sounds. I cursed. What difference did it make?

I went out to the kitchen, poured another big slug of bourbon—straight this time—and stood by the table looking down at the opened gift box containing the cigarette lighter. The whiskey helped, but it was still sickening as I began to probe through the mess with a stick, trying to classify the things that crawled out of it. Some were facts, some were assumptions, and some were mere guesses, but they all oozed off in the same direction. If the girl had been right about Roberts, you could at least assume she might be right about the rest of it. *You don't think he was the only one, do you*? And it was a cinch. It wasn't Roberts who tried to get her at the hotel in New Orleans. He was already dead.

I suddenly remembered trying to get her last night, with no success. Maybe the story about being out on Bourbon Street with the Dickinsons was as big a lie as the rest of it. And why had she checked out of the hotel so abruptly? According to the clerk, she still hadn't come in at five-thirty, but she was checked out and gone before seven, while she'd told me she was going to stay till Sunday. She hadn't received any phone call from here; she'd merely asked if there had been one, and when she learned there had, she'd packed and taken off.

I noticed again the letter from the broker's office sticking out from under the box the lighter had come in, and without quite knowing why, I slipped it out, tore open the envelope, and then stared uncomprehendingly at the typed verification form it contained. She had liquidated the account three days ago. Why? What had she needed $6000 for? We had a joint checking account here, and I never questioned the checks she cashed. I crushed it in my hand and threw it on the rug. It didn't matter. Roberts was what we were going to have out, and we'd do it before she got through this living room.

I glanced at my watch. The way she drove, she'd be here in less than an hour. Dropping the cigarette lighter in my pocket, I switched off the light and sat down to wait, conscious of the cold weight of anger in my chest and of the whiskey mounting to my head.

CHAPTER 3

FORTY MINUTES LATER GRAVEL CRUNCHED in the driveway beyond the far wall of the living room. I heard the garage door bang as it came up. The door closed.

The weight in my chest was so heavy now I could hardly breathe. Her key turned in the kitchen door. Light came on in the kitchen, and I heard the old magic tapping of high heels as she came toward the front of the house. Then she was silhouetted in the doorway, suitcase in one hand and her purse under her arm as she groped for the switch. The lights came on.

"Hello," I said. "Welcome home."

She gasped. The suitcase fell to the floor, followed by her purse. Then her eyes blazed with anger. "What are you sitting there in the dark for? You scared me half to death!"

She was very beautiful in anger, I thought—or any time, for that matter. She wore a slim dark suit and a white blouse, but she didn't have her coat. Maybe she'd left it in the car; she was as careless of mink as another woman might be of a housecoat.

"If this is your idea of a joke…" Her voice trailed off uncertainly as I still said nothing. "What's the matter? Aren't you glad to see me?"

"I want to know why you suddenly decided to come home," I said.

"Well, you wanted me to. But I must say, if this is the way you're going to act..."

"I want to know why," I repeated. She had come on into the room and started to peel off her gloves. She could make even that sexy and full of the promise of greater things to come. If she'd ever become a professional strip-teaser, I thought, she'd have the bald heads giving off wisps of steam by the time she started toying with the first zipper. It was obvious to her now that something was wrong, so I was about to get the good old laboratory-approved answer that answered everything. She gave me a sidelong glance. "Well! Do I have to have a reason?"

"I just wondered," I said, playing along with it.

"Maybe it was talking to you this afternoon," she murmured.

There was just enough pause for me to pick up my cue and join the act. All I had to do was stand up, take two steps toward her, and we'd be in bed in ninety seconds flat. And the hell of it was that once I started there'd be no more possibility of turning back than of changing my mind halfway down about going over Niagara Falls. Maybe she was a liar, and a cheat, and capable of using sex with the precise calculation of a tournament bridge player executing a squeeze play, but she was good at it. I reached in my pocket for the cigarette lighter and began tossing it in my hand.

She was still talking, probably to cover her bewilderment at this lack of response. "...Get so darned rumpled in a car." She twitched at the skirt, which was only slightly rump-sprung—and that by one of the shapeliest behinds this side of a barbershop calendar—and checked the stocking seams. The stockings, it appeared then, had to be pulled up. This might have seemed rather pointless in view of the fact that as soon as it penetrated my thick skull her delights were available now on a help-yourself basis; rather than having to wait while she rubbed cold cream on her face and had a sandwich and a glass of milk, the stockings were supposed to wind up on the bedroom floor along with assorted slips, garter belts, and panties—except of course that the act itself involved a great deal of unconscious skirt-raising and the revelation of rounded and satiny expanses of thigh above the tops of them. For her, this was admittedly crude, but maybe desperate situations called for desperate measures; when you had to probe the enemy across this type of terrain, you used only the battle-proven troops. She straightened, still talking, and gave me that half-pixie, half-inscrutable smile she does so well. "Does it seem awfully warm in here, or is it—is—?" Her voice faltered and trailed off to a stop. She'd seen the fighter.

"Is it what?" I asked politely.

She swallowed, licked her lips, and tried to go on, while her eyes grew wider and wider as they followed its course—up—down—up— "—is it just—just—?"

"Just you?" I asked. "I never thought of that, but I'll bet it is. And it's damned flattering too. It isn't often a husband gets this kind of testimonial."

She gasped. Her mouth dropped open, and a hand came up in front of it as if I were going to hit her from ten feet away. She backed up a step, her legs hit the sofa at the left of the dining room door, and she sat down. "I don't know—don't know what you mean."

"I mean it's heartwarming as hell when a girl who's shopped around over the neighborhood still feels an urge to come home for a good time. Unless, of course, you just dropped in to cash a check!" I began to break up in rage then. I stood up and started toward her.

She tried to get off the sofa and run. I threw her back, and pinned her there with a handful of blouse and bra. "What's the matter?" I asked thickly. "Don't you want to hear the news? Your boyfriend is dead."

She twisted and beat at my wrist, her eyes crawling with fear. "Have you gone crazy? Let me go!"

I leaned down in her face and shouted: "How long has this been going on?"

She drew up both feet, put them in my stomach, and kicked out like an uncoiling spring. There was the strength of desperation in it. The blouse tore. I lurched backward to keep my balance, hit the coffee table with the backs of my legs, and sprawled on the floor just past the end of it. She shot past me into the hall. I scrambled to my feet and tore after her. In the darkness I miscalculated the turn beyond the den and crashed into the wall. She had too much lead on me now, and just before I reached the bedroom door I heard it slam and then the click as she threw the night latch.

I crashed into it with my shoulder. It held. I hit it again, heard something start to give way, and the third time it flew open as the bolt tore off part of the door facing. I regained my balance, spun around, and groped for the light switch. She was nowhere in sight. Over to the left the door to the bath was closed. Just as I reached it, I heard the doorbell ringing in the front of the house. I twisted at the knob; it was locked. I backed up and hit it the way I had the other one, but nothing gave. I tried again; a throw rug skidded under my feet and I fell against the door with the point of my shoulder. My breath was whistling in my throat from rage and frustration. I kicked the rug out of the way and lunged at it again. She screamed. I was backing up to hit it once more when I finally became conscious that the doorbell was ringing continuously now. Some vestige of sanity returned. Whoever was out there would hear the uproar and call the police. "I'll be back!" I shouted through the door, and strode down the hall. When I switched on the porch light and yanked open the front door, I saw it was Mulholland, the beefy, handsome face looking mean under the shadow of his hat.

I was winded, and had to draw a breath before I could speak. "What do you want?"

"You," he said curtly.

"What do you mean 'you,' you silly bastard?" I snapped. "If you've got some reason for leaning on that doorbell, let's hear what it is."

"I'm taking you in. Scanlon wants you."

"What for?"

"Maybe you'll find out when you get there."

"Like hell. I'll find out now."

"Suit yourself." There was an eager and very ugly light in the greenish eyes. "He told me to bring you in, but he didn't say how. If you want to go in handcuffs, with a lump on your head, it's all the same to me."

"We'll see about that," I said. "Is he there now?"

"He's there."

I turned abruptly and went down the hallway to the living room. He followed me and stood in the doorway. I dialed the sheriff's office, and while I was waiting I saw he was looking toward the dining-room door. About half the suitcase showed beyond the end of the sofa, though her purse was out of sight from where he stood. He stuck a cigarette in his mouth, popped a match with his thumbnail the way he'd probably seen some tough type do it in the movies, and favored me with a nasty smile. "You wouldn't have been thinking of running out, would you?"

I stared at him contemptuously without bothering to answer. It occurred to me he was probably itching for a chance to belt me one and that I wasn't being very smart, but at the moment I was too full of rage to care. Scanlon answered the phone.

"Warren," I said. "What's this about wanting to see me?"

"That's right."

"What about?"

"Some questions I want to ask you."

"All right. It probably hasn't escaped your attention that I've lived in this town for 33 years, and there's a good chance I could find the courthouse without help. When you want to see me, I've got a telephone. So you can tell this farcical jerk you sent out here—"

"For crissake, if you've got to make a speech, could you do it tomorrow? Some of us would like to go home and get to bed."

"I'll be down the first thing in the morning."

"I want to see you right now." There was an ominous quietness in the way he said it.

There was no use arguing. "All right," I said savagely. "But next time don't be so ambiguous. Send three men and surround the house." I slammed down the receiver.

She'd probably be gone when I got back. Well, let her go, I thought numbly. What difference did it make now? It was obvious she was guilty, and there was nothing to be gained by any more fish-wife screaming at each other. Mulholland jerked his head. He went out the front. I threw on a topcoat, and hesitated, looking down the hallway toward the bedroom. Well, what was there to say? *Goodbye? It's been nice knowing you*? I turned, followed him out, and closed the door.

The county car was parked in the drive. Mulholland nodded curtly toward the front seat. I got in and lit a cigarette. The streets were deserted now, except for a few cars in front of Fuller's Cafe, and the wet pavement was shiny and black under the lights. The ropes of tinsel swayed, glittering coldly in the dark thrust of the wind. Why had she done it? It hurt, and went on hurting, and the wound only added to the cold weight of anger inside me. I pushed her off me and tried to think. The girl must have called Scanlon; there didn't seem to be any other explanation for this. And now that it seemed obvious her information was correct, I could be in serious trouble. A lot depended on whether or not she'd actually come forward and identified herself and produced the cigarette lighter; Scanlon wouldn't put much faith in an anonymous telephone call. Or would he? At the moment, my opinion of the county police force was unprintable.

The courthouse was dark now except for the sheriff's offices and a couple of windows on one of the upper floors where the custodian was working. Mulholland parked in front, and I got out without waiting for him, strode up the steps, and shoved through the swinging, rubber-flapped doors. I could hear his heels in the corridor behind me as I turned in the doorway. The big room was empty, but just as I came in Scanlon emerged from his private office. The shotgun was still on the desk. He nodded toward a chair at the corner of it. "Sit down."

I dropped the topcoat on the desk at my left, and sat down. Mulholland sprawled in the swivel chair behind another desk with his legs stretched out, watching me with what looked like amused satisfaction. Well, I'd get to him in a minute.

"I gather you had some reason for this?" I asked.

Scanlon took a cigar from his shirt pocket and bit the end off it. "That's right. I do."

"Good," I said. "So maybe if it's not classified information, I might even find out what it is."

Scanlon struck a match, holding it in front of his cigar while he went on staring at me. "I thought you'd heard. We're investigating a murder."

"And what have I got to do with it?"

"I didn't say you had anything to do with it. But you were out there at the time he was killed, and I want to hear your story again."

"Why?"

"I'll ask the questions. Did Roberts tell you he was going hunting this morning?"

"No." *Why had she done it?* My insides twisted. Scanlon said something else. "What?" I asked.

"But you recognized his car, when you parked at the end of the road, and knew he was in one of the blinds?"

So that was it. "I've told you three times," I said. "His car was *not* there when I parked. He came after I did."

It was obvious now the girl had called him. And also fairly obvious, on the other hand, that she hadn't identified herself. So he had the motive he'd lacked, if he believed it and could prove it. But without proof, he couldn't even mention it. Accusing another man's wife of infidelity on the strength of a crank telephone call could be risky even for a law-enforcement officer. So all he could do was accept the unsupported word of this telephoning creep and hammer at me with some oblique line of attack, hoping to trip me up. I wondered suddenly how much of this great zeal was due to the fact he already had one unsolved murder galling him. I was being made a goat. Rage came up into my throat and threatened to choke me.

I leaned forward over the desk. "Am I being accused of killing Roberts?"

"You're being questioned."

"Why?"

"I've told you—"

"You haven't told me anything. And until I'm told why I'm under suspicion, you can shove it."

He pounded a hand on the desk and pointed the cigar in my face, the gray eyes as bleak as Arctic ice. "Let's say you're under suspicion because you happened to be living in the same century when Roberts was killed. That's good enough for me, and it's good enough for you. If you want to play tough, I'll have you jugged as a material witness."

"Why don't you accuse me of killing Junior Delevan, while you're at it? It's only been a couple of years, and maybe you could clean out all your old files."

"Never mind Delevan!" he snapped.

"I also shot Cock Robin, and sank the Titanic—"

"Shut up."

"Can I use your telephone?"

He waved a hand toward the instrument. "Why?"

"I want to call the American consul," I said.

I dialed George Clement's house number. "Duke," I said, when he answered. "Can you come down to the sheriff's office for a minute?"

"Sure," he said. "But what's the trouble?"

"For some reason that nobody'll bother to explain, I seem to be suspected of murdering Dan Roberts—"

"But that's ridiculous—"

"My impression exactly. And I'd like some legal advice."

"I've just gone to bed, but I'll be there as soon as I can."

"Take your time. I can wait. And so can they." I hung up.

"You're acting like a damned fool," Scanlon snapped.

"I am a damned fool," I said. "I voted for you."

"You and Roberts pretty good friends?" he asked.

"I wouldn't say he was a close friend at all. He was an acquaintance. And a tenant."

"You ever have any trouble with him?"

I'd already answered that once, and saw no point in going into it again. I lit a cigarette and leaned back in the chair. "I have nothing to say."

"You mean you won't answer?"

"I mean I won't answer anything until I've been advised to by a lawyer. If you want to check that, ask me what time it is."

He slammed a hand on the desk. "You think I'm doing this for fun?"

"That's what puzzles me. I'd like to know myself."

We alternately glared and shouted at each other until George arrived in a little over ten minutes. He's 51, six feet tall, ramrod straight, with graying hair and a clipped gray mustache. At first glance he always strikes you as a little on the stuffy side, or at least over-correct, but he unbends when he knows you and he's a very astute lawyer and a deadly, if cautious, poker player. He's a passionate big-game fisherman, makes several trips to Florida or the Bahamas each year, and has two mounted sails and a dolphin in his offices, which take up a good part of the second floor of the Duquesne building. Fleurelle, his wife, is very wealthy, and the acknowledged leader of everything social in town, though it is my private opinion she has more than a trace of dragon blood and that George is pretty well policed. She's always regarded me as a roughneck.

George smiled and nodded to the others. "Good evening, Sheriff. Mr. Mulholland." He turned to me then. "Well, Hotspur, what seems to be the trouble?"

"I'm not sure myself," I said. "All I know is Scanlon sent this musical-comedy Gestapo agent to haul me out of bed—"

Everybody erupted at once. Mulholland started to get up as if he were going to take a swing at me. Scanlon waved him off curtly. "Sit down!"

"I've had a bellyful of this guy!" Mulholland snapped.

"Who hasn't?" Scanlon asked. "Anyway, there's no use your hanging around any longer. You might as well go home."

"Sheriff," George put in quietly, "maybe if I could speak to Duke alone for a moment—"

Scanlon ground out his cigar, rattling the ashtray. "Hell, yes. If you could knock some sense into that pig head, maybe we'd get somewhere."

Mulholland shucked off his gunbelt and holster, dropped them in a desk drawer, stared coldly at me, and stalked out. George and I moved over to one of the desks at the far corner of the room. I felt better now that he was here, and wondered if part of my anger had been merely to cover up the fact I was scared. We lighted cigarettes, and he said, "All right, let's have it."

I told him about the anonymous telephone call, and added, "So she probably called Scanlon too."

He nodded. "It seems likely. But he hasn't actually said so?"

"No. That's what burns me. He wouldn't dare admit he took any stock in a nut telephone call, but still he'd haul me down here and put me through the wringer. As far as I'm concerned, he can go to hell."

He shook his head with a wry smile. "Well, you're consistent, anyway. So far, you haven't done anything right."

"But, dammit, George—"

"No, you listen to me a minute. The girl, of course, is obviously a mental case, but no police officer worth his salt ever ignores any lead that comes up, no matter how tenuous. So Scanlon is obliged to check out her tip if he possibly can, even though he knows there's nothing to it. But instead of helping him eliminate it, so far you've done everything you could to convince him there might be some truth in it after all. Now stop acting like a wild boar with a toothache, or you *will* need a lawyer."

"You mean I could be charged with murder just on the strength of a poison telephone call and the fact I happened to be out at Crossman Slough when he was killed?"

"It's not likely, without some kind of proof, unless you keep insisting on giving the impression you've got something to hide. But there are a couple of other factors you've apparently overlooked. In the first place, Scanlon can make it very tough for you if you don't cooperate. Legally, too, and there's nothing I could do for you. With the weekend coming up, he could hold you without any charge at all until Monday. And in the second place, hindering the investigation by fighting him just makes it that much harder for him to find out who *did* kill Roberts, which— if you're under suspicion—is as much in your interest as it is in his. So stop acting like an adolescent and answer his questions; you have to, anyway, so you might as well do it gracefully. And for God's sake, stop riding Mulholland."

"What's he got to do with it?"

He sighed. "Hasn't it occurred to you that sending Mulholland to pick you up could have been deliberate? Scanlon's a smooth operator, and as brainy as they come, and the chances are he was trying to capitalize on that low flash-point of yours. A man who loses his temper is always more likely to say too much, or trip himself. Also, what Scanlon is trying to check is this hypothetical motive of jealousy; so behaving as if you were capable of unreasoning jealousy certainly isn't helping you much."

"Wait a minute!" I stared at him. "You mean, of Mulholland? Why would I be jealous of that posturing nitwit?"

"Face it, Duke; you've never liked him since he and Frances were in that Little Theatre play last spring. It's ridiculous, naturally, but you've gone out of your way to insult him."

"Nuts! I'd forgotten all about it."

He smiled and held up a hand. "All right, all right. Don't bite my head off. Just take my advice and cooperate with Scanlon. I'll stick around and drive you home."

"Should I say anything about the telephone call?"

"No. It's his problem; let him cope with it." He smiled, and you could see the well-oiled legal mind at work.

"Never deny an accusation that hasn't been made."

We went back to where Scanlon was waiting. Jealous of Mulholland, I thought scornfully. I hadn't even thought of that play for months.

CHAPTER 4

IT TOOK LESS THAN AN hour, and was a very relaxed interrogation. It was, in fact, too relaxed now; it was obvious he had realized this other approach was a mistake and was only going through the motions in order to justify getting me down here. He was marking time until he could get some proof or verification of that girl's story; when he had that, he'd land on me like a brick wall. I had to repeat the story of the whole morning, from my arrival at Crossman Slough and the blinds until the time I was back on the highway again on the way home, sometime around ten, and answer a lot of questions that were slanted to give the impression that what he was after was some detail I might have overlooked before, which would point to the third person who obviously had to be out there. Had I heard a car at any time? No. Had I *heard* anybody wading out to the blind where Roberts was? No. It was too far away, at least 150 yards. George sat at another desk, quietly smoking and taking no part in it.

At last, Scanlon rubbed a hand wearily across his face, and said, "Well, that's all, I guess." Then, as we were leaving, he tossed me a parting shot. "Looks as if the only lead to this is going to be the motive; we're not going to get anywhere until we find out *why* he was killed."

We went out and got into George's car. As we pulled away from the curb, he said, "Forget that telephone call, Duke. There's always at least one psycho in every town."

"I know," I said.

He turned into the cold desolation of Clebourne Street where the tinsel swayed and rustled in the wind. There was something reptilian about it. I had a splitting headache from the whiskey I'd drunk, and I was thinking of Frances again. She'd be gone now, and nobody knew she'd come home, but inevitably there was going to be talk when it was learned we were separated and being divorced. Scanlon would take a long hard look at it, but he couldn't prove it had been because of Roberts—not with what he had now. George turned right where the traffic light was blinking amber at the corner of Montrose, and drove the five blocks to the house in silence. When he pulled into the circular drive and stopped, he asked, "When will Frances be home?"

Not even George, I thought. "Sunday," I said. "Unless she changes her mind again."

"Fleurelle will be back Saturday." She was in Scottsdale, Arizona, visiting her sister. "We'd like to have you over for bridge next week."

"Sure," I said. "Thanks, counselor."

"Don't let this thing worry you. Scanlon'll clear it up eventually; the chances are a thousand to one it wasn't anybody from Carthage at all. Some enemy he made a long time ago, before he came here—which, incidentally, may have been the reason he was here in the first place. He was quite a ladies' man, I understand, and he might have made himself very unpopular with some husband or male relative somewhere."

"I suppose so," I said, and got out. "Good night, George."

"Good night." He swung on around the drive, and the red taillights disappeared in the direction we'd come. He lived in a big house on Clebourne on the east edge of town. I unlocked the front door, and went down the hallway to the living room. She'd left the light on. The suitcase and her purse were gone. I stood for a moment looking at the place where they had lain, feeling sick and empty as I had a mental picture of her grabbing them up and fleeing. It was a hell of a way for something to end. I could see her now, tearing the night apart with the Mercedes, like the ripping of cloth. To where? Back to New Orleans, and then to Nevada? More likely to Miami, I thought; that was where she was from, and Florida was as good a place as any to get a divorce. Well, I'd hear from her, or from her lawyer. I shrugged wearily and went out in the kitchen.

There was no hope of sleeping, so I filled the percolator, measured out the coffee, and plugged it in. When I went back to the living room I noticed idly that one of her gloves was lying on the sofa where she'd dropped it when I lunged at her. I'd seen it when I came in from the hall, but had paid no attention. The other was lying on the rug in front of the sofa. She'd been too scared and in too big a hurry to remember them when she'd gathered up the suitcase and purse. It was odd, though, that Mulholland hadn't seen them; he'd thought the suitcase was mine. Curious, I stepped over to the hall doorway where he'd been standing, and looked again. The sofa was Danish teak with pearl-gray cushions, the glove was black, and he would have been looking straight at it. Well, he was too busy admiring himself to notice anything.

I remembered then what George had said about my behaving as if I were jealous of him. Could people have actually believed that? I disliked him for the posing and arrogant jerk he was, but it went back a long time before the Little Theatre production of *Detective Story*, and had nothing to do with it. Anyway, there weren't many love scenes in the play, at least between McLeod and Mary McLeod, the two parts they'd had. I'd objected to her being in it, but only because of the long hours of rehearsals, five nights a week for over a month.

I paused, frowning...No, hell—she hadn't liked Mulholland herself; she thought he was a conceited ham, and I could remember her lying in bed laughing about the times he had blown up in his lines.

My own feeling about him was the result of a number of things, none of them having to do with Frances or the play. A couple of years ago he'd beaten up a sawmill hand and sent him to the hospital for no particular reason except that the boy was drunk and making a nuisance of himself and he, Mulholland, had an audience of admiring young punks in front of the drugstore. Any other officer would merely have arrested him and got him out of sight, but not our hero. I'd witnessed part of it, and with my usual tact I'd chewed him out and threatened to report him to Scanlon, with the result there'd been bad feeling between us ever since. He was a master of the calculated insolence of standing almost in your way along the sidewalk, so you had a choice of taking a half step aside in order to get around him or of bumping into him with the appearance of having done it deliberately. But jealous of him? Hah!

You don't think he was the only one, do you?

I cursed. Damn that girl, anyway! I tried to push the telephone call out of my mind, but it kept coming back. And I still didn't know why Frances had suddenly decided to come back from New Orleans. Did it have something to do with Roberts' death? But how could she have known of it? She hadn't received a phone call from here. No, I corrected myself; she merely hadn't received any at the hotel. She hadn't called me from there, had she?

I wished I could find out who the girl was. It was almost certain that I knew her. I stared at the telephone, wishing it would ring, and at the same time wondering why I thought she'd bother to call again; she'd gotten rid of her accumulation of poison for the day and was probably rucked cozily in bed sleeping the sleep of the just. She must be a girlfriend of Roberts'. I tried to remember any I'd seen him with, but came up with a blank. Being over 30 and married, I was completely out of touch with any crowd a single man Roberts' age would be likely to run around with. I suddenly thought of Barbara Ryan; she might know. As I reached for the telephone, I looked at my watch and saw with surprise it was one-fifteen. It was a sad time of night to wake anybody up, but maybe she wouldn't mind. She lived alone, in a small efficiency apartment about a block off Clebourne in the west end of town.

"Warren," I said when she answered. "I'm sorry to wake you."

"I wasn't asleep," she replied. "Just reading. And I'm glad you called. Is it really true, what they're saying now, that Roberts was killed by somebody?"

"There doesn't seem to be much doubt of it," I replied, and told her about the different sized shot.

"That's what I heard, but I just couldn't believe it. Who do they think did it?"

"No idea so far. But here's what I wanted to ask you—would you know anything about Roberts' girlfriends?"

She appeared to hesitate. Then she said guardedly, "Well, I'm no authority on the subject. Just what do you mean, Duke?"

"What girls he dated."

"Oh. Well, me for one. I've been out with him two or three times."

That was news to me. "What kind of guy was he?"

"Pleasant enough, good dancer, a little on the too-smooth side. He gave me the impression he took pretty good care of Dan Roberts."

"What do you know about any other girls?"

"Not much. I've seen him with one or two others at various times."

"Do you remember any of them?"

"Hmmm…Nadine Wilder…Midge Carson…I can't think of any others at the moment. Why?"

"I had a weird telephone call from a girl who wouldn't give her name, and I had a hunch she knew him pretty well."

"I see." There was that barely perceptible pause again, and then she added cynically, "Well, she could, quite fast, if she didn't watch her step."

"A wolf, then?"

"Operator is the word. Oh—about the two I named—if that telephone call was the usual sort people don't sign their names to, I doubt it was either of them. They're both pretty good kids. Nadine works for the power company—"

"And the Carson girl for Dr. Wyman," I said. "I know them both, and I don't think it was either. But if you remember any others, would you call me?"

"Sure thing. And if there's anything else I can do, just let me know."

"Thanks a lot." I hung up, and stood there for a moment wondering how many other people had heard rumors about Frances and Roberts. Those pauses hadn't been hard to read; she had a good idea what that girl had told me and was afraid of being backed into a position where she'd have to lie about it or confirm she'd heard the same thing.

My head was throbbing again. I went down the hallway to get some aspirin from the medicine chest in the bathroom. As I turned the corner beyond the den I saw there was a light still on in the bedroom, and I suddenly remembered the shattered door facing. I'd have to repair that before Malyina saw it; she'd wonder about it and talk. She was the colored girl who came in to do the housework twice a week, but she wouldn't be in again until Saturday; I could repair it tomorrow. Or today, I thought, remembering suddenly that it was Friday now. Maybe I could glue back the strip the bolt had torn off. But as I came nearer I saw it was too badly splintered and gouged; I'd have to replace it with a whole new facing and paint it. I'd been intent on the doorway and hadn't looked beyond it into the room itself, and now as I stepped inside I stopped in surprise. Her suitcase was on the bed. Beside it was another one, open, and a pile of dresses and underclothing.

Hadn't she taken anything with her? I looked stupidly around the room. The bed, a king-sized double over seven feet long, extended out from the right-hand wall, flanked on either side by closets, while directly opposite the doorway, in the rear wall, was the fireplace. The door to her dressing room and the bath, the one I'd failed to break in, was on the left, and open now, and just beyond it was a full-length mirror, opposite the foot of the bed. The only lights burning were the rose-shaded reading lamp on the far side and the one inside the dressing room, but as my glance swept across the mirror I caught the reflection of something dark on the floor on the other side of the bed. I came on into the room then, leaned over the corner of it, and looked squarely down into her face, or what was left of it.

My knees melted under me and I slid down onto the foot of the bed, clutching at the spread to keep from going on over the corner of it and falling on top of her. I kept opening and closing my mouth and swallowing to hold back the oily groundswell of nausea running up into my throat, and pressing my face into the bedspread as though I were convinced that if I could close my eyes tightly enough the picture would go away. Maybe it was the instrument itself that was the worst—or its position—the dirty, fire-blackened andiron lying across the column of her throat where he'd either dropped it or tossed it after he was through with it.

I turned the other way and tried to get up, but slid down and sat on the floor, facing the mirror, and for a second when I first saw it, I didn't even recognize my own face, greenish-white, staring, and shiny with sweat. My gaze started to slip downward to the reflected horror of what was on the other side of the bed, but I turned my head and tried again to get up. The telephone began to ring. There was an extension on the night table just beyond where she was lying, and the insistent clamor of it ran through my head like a whiter hot saw. I made it to my feet this time and walked unsteadily into the bathroom. Pulling down a large towel, I came back and managed to get it spread across her head and the upper part of her body. The telephone went on ringing.

She lay on her back, still fully clothed in the dark suit she'd worn when she came in except that her legs were twisted awkwardly and the skirt and slip were pulled halfway up her thighs, apparently from brushing against the bed as she fell. Still on my knees beside her, I caught the hem of the skirt and tried to pull it down without touching her, but when the leg moved and rearranged itself under the tugging, as if she were still alive, nausea hit me again and I had to turn away to keep from vomiting. It was the senseless brutality of it that was so sickening. Why had he beaten her in the face that way? I finally got the skirt pulled down, and stood up, still trembling, and wiped the sweat from my face.

The closet door, between the night table and the rear wall, was open. Apparently she had been taking clothes from it, and when her back was turned he'd lifted the andiron from the fireplace and hit her the first time, the blow that crushed the top of her skull. Her right hand and lower arm extended from under the edge of the towel; I knelt again and looked at them, and then raised the corner of the towel to examine the left. Neither was broken, and there were no bruises, or any soot, on them; she hadn't raised her arms to try to protect herself, so definitely he'd hit her the first time from behind. That blow would have killed her instantly, and the rest of it was sheer sadism or some pathological hatred you could only guess at.

But she must have let him in; I'd locked the front door when I left, and the others were already locked. I became aware then that something had changed in the room, but it was a second or two before I realized what it was. The telephone had finally quit ringing. I turned to it and picked up the receiver, still numb with shock, and started to dial the sheriff's office. With a nervous giggle that was near the borderline of hysteria, I was conscious of thinking it was lucky for me I was in the sheriff's office, with witnesses, when it happened. Then I stopped, and let the receiver fall back on the cradle. I was staring with horror at the splintered door frame.

Mr. Mulholland will please take the stand...

I rang the doorbell for a long time ... Yes, it was at least five minutes ... When he finally did answer, he was all out of breath, and crazy-acting, and wild-eyed. I could smell the liquor on him ... Yes, that's the same suitcase. I just thought at the time it was his...

Wait! The suitcase was in the living room when I left. He'd have to testify there was no chance I could have moved it, because I came out the door right behind him. So it would be obvious she was still alive then—I stopped. What a defense that would be! By now I'd already been here at least twenty minutes, alone, since George had let me off in front of the house.

I'd told George she was still in New Orleans, when she was already dead here in the bedroom. Friend or not, he'd still have to testify.

They already had the motive. The girl had given them that.

The telephone started to ring again.

... and so, ladies and gentlemen of the jury, having already killed his wife's lover, he learned from her hotel in New Orleans that she was on her way home, waylaid her in the living room ... where she dropped her suitcase, fled in terror to the bedroom and, in a last and futile attempt to save her life, bolted the door...

... I give you this andiron ... these monstrous photographs ... who but a man inflamed to madness by the goadings of a cancerous and unreasoning jealousy...

I had to do something.

Yes, *what*? I heard my voice saying it aloud, and then that nervous giggle again, warning me how near I was to breaking up completely into hysteria.

Maybe if I got out of this room where her scream was still ringing in my ears I could think. But it wasn't a scream, I told myself; it was only the telephone. I went down the hall with it ringing behind me in the bedroom and ahead of me in the living room, as if I were running wildly and forever just to stay in one place on a treadmill in some ultramodern Hell filled with shrilling telephones all trying to drive me over the brink into madness. Then in a moment of lucidity, like a sun-filled hole in a drifting curtain of fog, it occurred to me that if I answered it the damned thing would stop. But as I came into the living room it stopped anyway. I went on to the kitchen, only half conscious of what I was doing, and from force of habit poured a cup of coffee from the percolator which had shut itself off now. I was raising it to my lips when I saw her face again, and dropped the whole thing, cup, saucer, and all, into the sink. I turned on the tap and let the water run, splashing among the fragments of china, while I cupped trembling hands and caught some to wash my face. I didn't know why. Maybe I thought it would clear my head. I dried my face on a dish towel, dropped it on the edge of the sink, and sat down at the breakfast table to fumble for a cigarette.

Mother of God! Darrow come back from the grave couldn't save me.

Fragments of thought went whirling through my mind, too jumbled and disconnected to make sense or form any recognizable pattern. It had to be Mulholland. No one else had even known she was home. He *had* seen the glove, and knew all the time the suitcase was hers. Then he must have killed Roberts, and she was mixed up in it some way—No, I thought then, it didn't have to be Mulholland; it could still be anybody. She'd let the man into the house, so it followed she could also have called him and told him she was home, the minute I was out the door.

And what had she really been doing in New Orleans? What had she needed all that money for? I sprang up and ran back to the bedroom, looking wildly around for her purse; there might be something in it, some kind of information. How did I know she was even in New Orleans today, or last night? She hadn't got back to the hotel to check out until sometime between five-thirty and seven P.M.; she could even have been here in Carthage. I spotted her purse on the bed beside the two suitcases, pulled it open, and began pawing through the litter women carry around with them—lipstick, comb, mirror, car keys, tissues, handkerchief. There was nothing here. Wait—receipted hotel bill, with her credit card number. December to January 5th. That was right. I opened her billfold. It held two fives, and three ones.

She'd had six hundred in cash when she left here, and presumably had cashed a check for five hundred today, she'd sold stocks worth six thousand, she'd paid the hotel bill by credit card, and she had thirteen dollars. Good God. Then I remembered she hadn't been wearing her coat when she came in, one of those light shades of mink that had cost around four thousand. I ran back to the kitchen, yanked open the door to the garage, and looked in the Mercedes. There was no coat in it.

I came back to the living room and stood by the desk, staring blankly at the slip from the broker's office, still dazed and only half conscious of what I was doing. What did it all mean? What had she done with it? Then my head cleared a little, and I wondered savagely what difference it made. The question was what I was going to do. Call the police? Run? Call George, and tell him? Then I went rigid with fear. Tires crunched on the gravel in front. I heard a car door slam, and then footsteps on the porch. The doorbell sounded. It rang again before I could even move. Sweat broke out on my face as I tiptoed to one of the front windows, parted the drapes a fraction of an inch, and peered out. It was a police car, the red light flashing in the darkness.

It was too late to run. Even if I could get the garage door open without his hearing me, his car was blocking the drive. I could get out the back on foot, but where would I go? They'd run me down in an hour. I couldn't see the man in front of the door, but it must be Mulholland. The bell rang again, three or four angry, insistent bursts, then a fist pounded on the panel. If I didn't let him in, he'd break it down. I took a deep breath, trying to get air past the tightness in my chest, and walked down the hall.

It was Len Owens, the night deputy. He looked faintly sheepish. "Sorry to disturb you, Mr. Warren—"

My mouth opened. Nothing came out, so I closed it.

"We had a call from Mrs. Ryan," he went on. "She was pretty upset. She said she'd just been talking to you on the phone, and then called back a few minutes later and couldn't get an answer."

I managed a smile, wondering if he could hear the noise my face made as it split. "I was—uh—lying down, and must have dozed off. I guess that was it. I must have been asleep." Now that I had finally achieved speech, I couldn't seem to shut myself off.

"I guess everybody's a little jumpy, with that thing about Roberts. Anyway, if you'd just call her back." He started to turn away.

You could tell him now, I thought. It's only been a half hour. *Oh, by the way—my wife's just been murdered too. I mean—since you're here, you might as well have a look. Sure.*

"Good night, Mr. Warren." He stepped down off the porch and walked back toward the car.

I've been meaning to call you, but what with one thing and another—you know how it is.

"Good night." I closed the door and collapsed against it like the heroine of a 1923 movie. The car drove off. I could never report it now.

CHAPTER 5

SHE WAS APOLOGETIC. "I felt silly, sending the police to check, but when I called right back, twice—and after that terrible thing with Roberts—"

"It's all right," I said. The numbness of shock was wearing off now and my mind was operating a little better. "I must have dropped off to sleep. What was it?"

"Well, not important enough to cause all that uproar. But you asked me to call you back if I remembered any other girls Roberts had dated."

"You've thought of another one?"

"No. Not yet. But I was going to suggest you try Ernie Sewell. He's worked for Roberts ever since he opened the store, and probably knows him as well as anybody in town. Also, Roberts would be more likely to discuss his conquests with another man than he would with a new prospect. He was no high-school type."

I should have thought of Sewell myself. "Thanks. That's a good idea. And there was something else I wanted to ask you. When Frances called me this afternoon, do you remember whether the operator actually said New Orleans, or just long distance?"

Some people might have asked, "Why?" but not Barbara Ryan. She'd worked for me for over a year, but I was just now beginning to appreciate her. "I'm not sure now," she said. "All I remember is that it was from a pay phone."

"Hold it! Are you sure of that?"

"Yes. The line was open all the way, and I distinctly remember the operator telling her how much money to deposit."

I'm still lying here in bed—What was the object of a pointless falsehood like that? A pathological compulsion to lie? And where did the trumpet come in? Well, maybe it was a jukebox.

"How much was it?" I asked.

"Hmmm. Ninety cents, I think. Yes, that's right."

Then it could have been New Orleans. It was a cinch it wasn't local. I yanked my thoughts back on the track. An idea was beginning to take form in my mind, but I was going to need help—help from somebody very smart and somebody I could trust. George would fill the bill on both counts, but I couldn't ask him; his professional code of ethics wouldn't allow him to be a party to anything unorthodox and probably illegal, even if he knew I was innocent. He'd simply tell me to call the police. Barbara could do it, if she would, and if I could figure out a way to keep from implicating her.

"Listen," I said, "I can't explain now, but in the morning Scanlon is probably going to be asking you a lot of questions about me. Answer everything he asks, fully and truthfully, except don't tell him I asked you or even mentioned it. Got it?"

"Well, it sounds simple enough in an incomprehensible sort of way; I think I can swing it. Anything else?"

"If he should ask if anything's missing from the safe in the office, inventory it, and tell him. That's all. And thanks a million, Barbara."

I hurried back to the bedroom. Avoiding the other side of the bed and being careful not to disturb anything I didn't have to, I quickly changed into a dark suit, fresh shirt, and tie, and hauled one of my own suitcases out of the closet on this side, a tan leather two-suiter with my initials stamped on it. I threw in a suit, several shirts, changes of underwear, and the toilet kit with the spare electric razor, and just before I closed the bag it occurred to me a picture would help. The only photograph I'd ever been able to persuade her to have made was the wedding picture; it would have to do. I swung around to the dresser to pick it up, and stared blankly. It was gone.

It was impossible. It'd been there just—I stopped, aware I couldn't remember when I had seen it last. I was so accustomed to its being there, it might have been a week since I'd actually noticed it. Maybe Malvina had moved it. I yanked open drawers, and looked on the dressing table in the bath. It had vanished. She'd never liked it, so maybe she destroyed it, though I was certain I must have seen it since she left. I swore nervously. This was wasting precious time; I couldn't stand here doddering like an old man. I had a small copy of the same photograph in my wallet; it would have to do. I slammed the suitcase shut, hit the light switch, and went down the hall. Grabbing the topcoat and a hat, I killed the rest of the lights, and slipped out the kitchen door into the garage.

I tossed the bag into the Chevrolet, and eased up the big overhead door. The street was deserted and dark beyond the driveway. I backed out and closed the door. The only way to do it was as naturally as possible, I thought. This time of night it would be very easy to tell whether I was being followed, and especially by the police. The County cars and the two owned by the city police were all marked. I turned left one block before Clebourne, drove west on Taylor for three blocks, turned right on Fulton to come out into Clebourne just west of the office, the way I always drove to work. Clebourne Street is quite wide, and still has angle parking. I slid into a space in front of the office and got out. Three cars were parked in front of Fuller's, just to my left, but none of them was a police car. The tinsel made a scaly, rustling sound in the wind as I stepped across the sidewalk and unlocked the door. There was nobody in sight along the sidewalk.

The big fireproof safe was against the back wall, between the door leading into my office and the one going back to the washroom and the rear entrance on the alley, but a light was always left on it so it was in full view of the street. I walked straight back to it, fighting an impulse to look over my shoulder at the windows, knelt, and began turning the knob through the combination. The last tumbler fell in place. I pulled the door open, took out my keys, unlocked the steel door inside, and slid out the brown Manila folder I wanted. It contained something over $18,000 in matured Series E bonds, mostly 500-and 1000-dollar denominations. I closed the safe, spun the knob, and before I turned around I took out a cigarette and lit it. There was nobody in sight beyond the windows. I went out and locked the door.

I was just backing the Chevrolet away from the curb when a police car came around the corner from Fulton behind me. For an instant I felt a quick stab of fear; then I saw it was only Cap Deets, the night patrolman, in one of the city cars. He waved, and went on past. My only danger at the moment was Scanlon, in case he was having me watched to see if I tried to leave town. Or Mulholland, I thought grimly, if he were the one who'd killed her. I drove on down Clebourne at a casual pace and turned right onto Montrose as if I were going home. There was nobody behind me. Two blocks over I turned right again and was headed back parallel to Clebourne. When I reached the west end of town I cut back to Clebourne and the highway, checked the mirror once more, and breathed softly in release of tension as I bore down on the accelerator. When I passed the service-club signs at the city limits I was doing 70.

It was six-twenty and just growing light when I parked the car in a lot at the New Orleans airport. I was hollow-eyed with fatigue and the nervous strain of sustained highspeed driving with one eye cocked on the mirror for the Highway Patrol, but still keyed up mentally as I put the packet of bonds in the suitcase, locked the car, and carried the bag into the terminal. I had a cup of coffee at the lunchroom, asked the cashier for some change, and headed for a telephone booth, setting the suitcase down where I could watch it through the door.

I dialed the long-distance operator and put in a person-to-person call to Ernie Sewell. I didn't know his number, but he lived on Springer Street, on the edge of town, in a small ranch-style house he and his wife were paying off. She worked for the county, in the Tax Assessor's office. He was a serious-minded and hardworking young man of about 24 who'd been a track and basketball star in high school, and had been in charge of the sporting-goods department at Jennings Hardware before he went to work for Roberts.

"Hello?" he said sleepily. "Oh. Mr. Warren? I thought the operator said New Orleans."

"She did," I said. "I came down last night. I'm sorry to get you out of bed this early."

"It's all right. Matter of fact, I was going to call you today. But I won't bother you about it now, over long distance."

"Go ahead," I said. "What is it?"

"Well," he replied hesitantly, "it's about the store. I don't want to sound like a ghoul, with Roberts not even buried yet, but somebody's going to buy the stock and fixtures, probably one of those bankruptcy outfits. My idea is that since you own the building you'd rather have the store there than the vacant space. All I've got is a few hundred dollars saved up, but I thought maybe if you'd put in a word for me at the bank I might be able to swing it. Run right, that place could make money."

"You mean it didn't? I thought Roberts was doing all right."

"Well, that's the funny part of it; it seemed to make money, and maybe the books'll show a big profit, but I wouldn't want to try to get the loan under false pretenses. The truth is we didn't move enough merchandise to make anything after he paid the rent and my salary. The potential's there, all right, or I wouldn't want it, but he just didn't seem to have any interest in the place, and he wouldn't give me any authority to speak of. For one thing, he'd never keep his stock up; he wouldn't order anything until somebody asked for it, and then it's too late—they'd just go to Jennings. And I couldn't get him to advertise."

"I see," I said, thinking of that Browning shotgun, and the Porsche, and a thousand-dollar membership in the Duck Club. "How'd he keep going?"

"I don't know, so help me, Mr. Warren. He never seemed to have any trouble meeting his bills, and he always had a good-sized balance at the bank. But I do know that if somebody took hold of that place who knew how to run a sporting-goods store and would stay home and run it, he could have Jennings looking at his hole card inside of three months. He hasn't got anybody over there that knows anything about guns and fishing tackle."

"I know," I said. "Then you think Roberts was doctoring his books, or had some other source of income?"

"Well, I don't know whether he was faking the books or not, but he sure seemed to be banking more money than we took in.

I realize it'd be easier to get the loan if I didn't say anything about this, but I don't like to do business that way."

"I'll see you get the loan," I said. "But what about Roberts' family? Have they located anybody yet?"

"Yes. Mr. Scanlon and I went down to the store yesterday evening after supper and found a couple of letters with his brother's address on them. He lives in Houston, Texas. Scanlon sent off a wire, and got one back in a couple of hours. The brother's making arrangements to have the body shipped to Houston for the funeral. It'll be a week or ten days, though, before he can get down here to pick up Roberts' personal stuff and see about disposing of the store."

"Do you remember the brother's address?"

"No, I'm sorry. I do remember his name was Clinton, though. Clinton L. Roberts."

"You won't open the store today, I suppose?"

"No. Scanlon said we'd better close it until the brother gets here. All his stuff is there in the apartment in back. I turned the key over to him—Mr. Scanlon, I mean."

"I see. Well, here's what I wanted to ask you, Ernie. Do you happen to know what girls Roberts ran around with mostly?"

By now he was probably exploding with curiosity, but he was too polite to express it. "Well, there were a lot of 'em, I guess, though he never talked about 'em much. He was more interested in girls than he was in the store, that's for sure. At different times I've seen him with Carol Holliday, and Mrs. Ryan that works for you, and Midge Carson. And let's see—Doris Bentley, and Sue Prentiss. And probably some more I can't think of at the moment."

Doris Bentley, I thought. She'd worked for Frances when she had the dress shop. It'd been a year and a half since I'd heard her voice on the telephone, but in those days she'd answer quite often when I'd call there for Frances. It could be—

"Thanks a lot, Ernie," I said. "And don't worry about the loan."

I carried the bag out front, mingled with a crowd of incoming passengers reclaiming their luggage, and took the airport bus downtown. At the first stop, I got off, took a taxi to a cheap hotel off the lower end of Canal Street, and registered as James D. Weaver, of Tulsa, Oklahoma. It was twenty after seven, still two hours before the banks opened. The room was on the second floor, overlooking a dreary alley filled with utility poles and trash barrels. I left a call for nine-thirty, and lay down. The bed rocked as if I were still driving, and the instant I closed my eyes the pulpy and battered mass of her face was burned into the backs of the lids down to the last projecting shard of bone, and I sat up shaking and sick, my mouth locked against the outcry welling up inside me.

Sleep was out of the question. I shaved and took a shower, and sat on the side of the bed, chain-smoking cigarettes until almost nine, trying to fit the pieces of the puzzle into some recognizable pattern. It was hopeless. I didn't have enough of them. Taking the folder from the suitcase, I walked uptown through chill sunlight and the early morning traffic to a bank where one of the officers knew me, and turned in the bonds. It was a routine procedure until they asked whether I wanted a cashier's check or a draft and I explained I wanted it in cash. It was obvious they disapproved and thought I had a screw loose somewhere, but they had to give it to me. I made some lame excuse about a business deal, stowed the 180 one hundred-dollar bills and some change in my wallet and the inside pockets of my jacket, and went out. It was ten-ten A.M. now, and I had to work fast.

I always ate breakfast at Fuller's, even when Frances was home, because she never got up before ten. I was usually in the office by eight-fifteen. At least six mornings of the week Mulholland was there having his breakfast at the same time, and even if he missed today he'd probably ask if anybody had seen me. At any rate, by this time Scanlon would have learned that I hadn't shown up so in town. He'd call the office, and the house, while the air around the courthouse became incandescent with profanity, and within a few minutes somebody was going to be checking the garage at home to see if my car was gone. When they found it missing, but the Mercedes there, and still could get no answer, they'd break in a door, and within an hour the police all the way from Texas to South Carolina were going to have the description and license number of that Chevrolet. Ernie might call and tell him I was in New Orleans, as soon as the story got around town, but whether he did or not, by sometime this afternoon he'd have found out where I cashed the bonds and they'd have located the car abandoned at the airport. I had four or five hours at the most.

I headed for a phone booth, and began flipping through the yellow pages of the directory. *Dentists... Derricks... Desks...*

Louis Norman of the Norman Detective Agency had a lean and thoughtful face, the attentive gaze of a born listener, and some quality of ageless disillusion about the eyes which seemed to promise that if you hoped to tell him anything that would surprise him you were out of luck. He leaned back in his chair with a ruler balanced between his fingertips and surveyed me across the top of it. "What can I do for you, Mr.—?"

"Warren." I passed over one of my business cards. "John D. Warren, Carthage, Alabama. First, have you got enough men to handle a rush job that'll probably take a lot of legwork?"

He nodded. "Three, beside myself, and I can get a couple more if necessary. That kind of crash job can run into money, though, if it takes very long."

"I know." I slid six one hundred-dollar bills from the overstuffed wallet and dropped them on the desk in front of him. "Use your own judgment as to how many men you need. If it runs more, bill me. I want some information, and I want it fast."

"That's the business we're in. What is it you need?"

While I had the wallet out, I removed the photograph of Frances and dropped it beside the money. "That's my wife. She was in New Orleans from December 30th until yesterday. I want to know the places she went, whom she was seeing, and what she was doing."

"You say until yesterday. Then she's not here now?"

"No. She's at home."

He pursed his lips. "It won't be easy. Tailing is one thing; backtrailing—"

"If it were easy, I wouldn't need professionals," I said. "Can you do it?"

"Probably. How old is the picture?"

"Eighteen months. It's a good likeness."

"That'll help. But a lot would still depend on what kind of starting point you can give us." He reached for a pad and undipped his pen.

"Full name, Frances Warren," I said. "Maiden name, Frances Kinnan. Twenty-seven years old, five-feet-seven, about 120 pounds, black hair, blue-green eyes. Always expensively dressed, in good taste, and in daytime she favors dark tailored suits. When she came down here she had a light-colored mink coat, but sometime in the seven days it apparently disappeared—along with about seven thousand dollars in cash. She was driving a dark blue Mercedes-Benz 220 sedan with blue upholstery and Alabama license plates, but the chances are she didn't use it getting around the city because she doesn't like driving in heavy traffic and trying to outguess these one-way streets. So she would have been using taxis, because she never walks anywhere if she can help it and wouldn't be found dead on a bus or streetcar. Any taxi driver would remember her, because of the legs if nothing else, and the fact she's a lousy tipper and arrogant enough to take back the dime if he got unhappy about it. She was registered at the Devore Hotel, and checked out yesterday around seven P.M.

"She came down originally to go to the Sugar Bowl game with some New Orleans friends, the Harold L. Dickinsons of 2770 Stilwell Drive. She and Mrs. Dickinson were supposed to have gone to a series of concerts during the past week, and some cocktail parties, but as to how much she actually saw of the Dickinsons I don't know. You might be able to find out something there, without mentioning me. I do know she was at the hotel at least part of the time, because I talked to her there on the nights of January 2nd and 3rd—"

He interrupted. "Did you call her, or she call you?"

"I called her," I said. "She was at the hotel, all right."

"Just what makes you suspect her?"

I explained about the call from the pay station when she said she was at the hotel. "And there's the money, of course. Nobody could run through $7000 in a week going to a football game and a couple of concerts. Or even buying clothes—unless she was in Paris. And, also, what happened to the coat?"

"Was it insured?"

"Yes."

"Even so, it might have been lost or stolen and she was afraid to tell you. But with all the other money she seems to have got rid of, it seems more likely she sold it or hocked it. I'll have a man hit the pawn shops and check back through the classified ads. But how did she get hold of $7000? You don't carry that much in a checking account, do you?"

I explained about the stocks she'd sold, and gave him the name of the broker.

He nodded. "Then if it was hers, it's not the money you're interested in?"

"No," I said. "Only what she was doing with it."

"You believe it's another man?"

"Sure. I can't think of any other reason she'd lie about where she was. And she must have given that money to somebody."

"This is professional," he said, "so don't take offense. Strictly off that photograph, she'd never have to buy any men, so there must be another answer. Has she ever, to your knowledge, been in any kind of trouble? Anything she could be blackmailed for?"

"No," I said. "She was no gangster or gun moll. Before we were married, she owned a dress shop in Carthage. And before that, she ran one in Miami."

"Does she have family connections of any kind in Carthage?"

"No," I said.

"Friends? I mean, before she came there?"

"No."

"Hmmm. Did she ever say why she gave up a business in a city the size of Miami to open one in a small town where she didn't even know anybody?"

"Sure. It was a divorce. She and her husband owned the place jointly, and when they split up they sold it and divided the proceeds." I explained how she was on her way to the Coast when she stopped overnight in Carthage and became interested in its possibilities.

"I see," he said, though it was obvious he wasn't completely satisfied, any more than I was now. "Where can I get in touch with you here?"

"You can't. I'm just in town for the day, and haven't got a hotel room. But I'll call you this afternoon, and after that you can reach me at my office in Carthage. The number's on the card. If I'm not in, you can give the information to my secretary, Mrs. Barbara Ryan."

He gave a shake of the head. "We don't like to pass confidential information to a third person."

"It's all right in this case," I said. "I authorize it."

"You'll have to put that in writing. And there's another thing—she'll have to identify herself. Any woman on the phone could say her name was Barbara Ryan."

"Yes, I know. But you can give me a file number."

"All right," he agreed reluctantly. He scribbled something on the pad. "The number is W-511."

"Right." I made a note of it, scribbled the authorization on another sheet of his pad, and signed it. When I went out, he was already giving orders on the intercom.

I stopped at a bank, got twenty dollars worth of quarters and dimes, and took a taxi to the telephone company office. In the battery of out-of-town directories, I looked up detective agencies in Houston and Miami. One of the big nationwide outfits could have handled all three jobs, but I had to keep them separate.

Selecting an outfit called Crosby Investigations in Miami and a man named Howard Cates in Houston, I wrote down the addresses and phone numbers and headed for a booth. I put in the call to Miami first, person-to-person to Crosby himself. He was in. I introduced myself, and asked, "Can you handle a rush job that'll take a couple of men?"

"Yes, sir."

"Good. I'll mail you a cashier's check for a retainer within the next half hour, airmail special, and you should have it this afternoon. Is $200 all right?"

"Sure thing, Mr. Warren. What is it you want?"

"A confidential check on an employee who used to live in Miami. Her name's Frances Kinnan." I gave him a description. "She was born in Orlando, in 1934, went to high school there, and attended the University of Miami for two years, according to the information on her personnel card. Around 1953 she went to work as a salesgirl in the women's-wear section of Burdine's, and later became assistant to the head of the advertising department. In 1955 she married a man named Leon Dupre who'd been some kind of minor executive with one of the dress shop chains— Lerner's, I think—and the two of them opened a shop on Flagler Street. It was called Leon's, and specialized mostly in resort clothes. In 1958, she and Dupre were divorced, and they sold out. That should be enough information for you to pick up the trail, and what I want to know specifically is whether she's ever been in any kind of trouble, if there actually was a divorce, where Dupre is now—if possible—and if she ever knew a man named Dan Roberts." I gave him a description of Roberts. "Can you handle it?"

"With that much to start on, it'll be easy. How much time do we have, and how do you want the report? By mail?"

"No. Wire it to me at my office in Carthage. By five P.M. tomorrow at the latest."

"We'll do it, or break a leg."

I hung up, dialed the long-distance operator again, and put in the call to Houston. Cates' line was busy and I had to wait five minutes and try again. This time I got him. I told him my name and address, made the same arrangement for payment I had with Crosby, and asked for a report on Roberts. "I don't know where he lived in Houston," I said, "or how long ago he moved away, but he still has a brother living there. The brother's name is Clinton L. Roberts, and he should be in the book, for a place to start."

"That'll do," he said. "And just what is it you want to know?"

"What business he was in there, whether he's ever been in trouble with the police, why he left, whether he has any known enemies, and whether he's ever lived in, or been in, Florida. Wire it to me at my office, not later than tomorrow afternoon if you can swing it. Okay?"

"Right. We can do it."

I went out. At another bank I bought the two cashier's checks, ducked into a drugstore for airmail envelopes, addressed them and marked them special delivery, and plastered on a bunch of stamps from the vending machine. Dropping them in a mailbox, I headed out Rampart, looking at cheap used cars on lots decorated with whirling orange-colored propellers. It was nearly one P.M. now, and I was beginning to feel naked on the street. Picking out an accessory-cluttered and fox-tailed old 1950 Olds, I gave my name as Homer Stites of Shreveport, paid cash for it, and drove it back uptown to a parking lot.

I took a taxi back to the hotel, checked out, and carried the suitcase up the thronged sidewalks of Canal Street, cut over to the parking lot, and locked it in the trunk of the car. It was two-fifteen P.M. I couldn't wait any longer; any time now the police would have men covering the bus station, railroad terminals, and the airport, and they'd know I couldn't have got away after that. I ducked into a phone booth and called Norman.

CHAPTER 6

"OH," HE SAID. "I wasn't expecting you quite so soon."

"I won't be able to stay in town as long as I'd thought," I explained. "Have you come up with anything yet?"

"Not much. The man working the hock shops hasn't got any lead on the coat so far, but I had a call about twenty minutes ago from Snyder, who's covering the Devore Hotel. So far, of course, all he's been able to talk to is the day-shift crew, but he has uncovered one or two items. Several bellmen and the doorman remember seeing her in the coat from time to time when she first checked in, but nobody recalls seeing it in the last two or three days. If it was lost or stolen, though, she never reported it to anybody in the hotel or to the police, as far as we can find out. According to the housekeeper on her floor, she stayed in her room every night, and if she ever had a man there nobody ever saw him and he didn't leave any tracks. She apparently had no visitors at all, and the only phone calls anybody can remember were from a woman, probably Mrs. Dickinson. There is one funny thing, though; she was never in the hotel in the afternoon. She always left a call for ten-thirty A.M., had breakfast and the newspapers sent up to her room, and then went out about a quarter of one. The doorman always got her a cab, but he never heard what she told the driver.

We've had the picture copied, and at shift-changing time at four P.M. we'll cover the garages of all three leading cab companies to catch as many of the day-shift jockeys as we can at one time. There's a good chance we'll find somebody who remembers her and where he took her."

"Good," I said. "And thanks a lot. I'll be in touch."

"We'll have something definite by tomorrow morning, I'm pretty sure." He hesitated, and then went on, "Look, Mr. Warren, it's your business, and you don't have to tell us if you don't want to, but it'll make it a lot easier if you level with us. Were you having her tailed at any time when she was down here?"

I frowned. "No. Of course not. Why?"

"Well, I've got a hunch somebody else was interested in what she was doing."

"Why?"

"Well, these bellmen are a pretty wise bunch, and they don't miss much. One of 'em hinted he knew something, and when Snyder primed him with an extra fin, he said there was a guy he was pretty sure followed her away from the hotel three or four times. He'd come in around noon and stooge around the lobby chewing a cigar and pretending to read a paper, and when she'd come out of the elevator he'd drift out after her and take the next cab off the stand."

"You suppose the kid just made it up, for the five bucks?"

"There's a chance, of course, but I don't think so. From the way he described this joker, I think I know who he is. He's in the business."

"Could you find out who hired him?"

"Not a chance. If it's the guy I think it is, he wouldn't tell his mother the way to a fire exit."

"Could the police make him talk?"

"Sure, or make him wish he had. But you've got nothing to take to the police, at least so far. There's no law against her spending her own money—or even yours, for that matter."

"Yeah," I said. I wondered what his face would look like when he saw the evening papers. "Well, keep digging."

I hung up, dug in my pocket for another handful of change, and dialed long-distance. "I want to put in a person-to-person call to L. S. MacKnight, of the MacKnight Construction Co., El Paso, Texas."

"Thank you. Will you hold on, please?"

Mac was an old friend. We'd gone to the same military school in Pennsylvania and later were classmates at Texas A&M. We hunted quail together somewhere every year. I hoped he was in the office now. Luck was with me.

"Duke? Why, you crazy devil, where are you?"

"New Orleans."

"Well, grab some airplane. Let's go huntin'."

"I wish I could, but at the moment I'm working the other side of the street."

"What do you mean?"

"I'm in a jam, and I need a little help."

"Name it, pal."

"Well, look, I'd better tell you first—you could get your tail in a sling, if they ever proved it—"

He cut me off. "I said name it, knucklehead. Never mind the fine print."

"I want you to send a telegram for me."

"Hell, is that all?"

"It's enough. Let's see—you're on Mountain Time there, so send it about eight tomorrow morning, straight wire. Phone it in

71

from a pay phone, so there's no way they can trace it back to you. Got a pencil handy?"

"Right. Commence firing."

"TO WARREN REALTY COMPANY, CARTHAGE, ALABAMA. IMPERATIVE YOU CONTACT LOUIS NORMAN AGENCY NEW ORLEANS PHONE CYPRESS FIVE EIGHT THREE TWO SEVEN REGARDING PENDING DEAL FILE NUMBER W-511 REPEAT WILLIAM FIVE ONE ONE STOP WILL CALL YOU LATER SIGNED WEAVER."

"Check." He read it back. "Anything else I can do?"

"No," I said. "*Gracias, amigo.*"

"*Por nada.* How bad is this thing, pal?"

"Real bad."

"Okay. I'm holding it."

"Hang on." I dropped the receiver back on the hook, and walked back to the parking lot. The old car ran all right. Beyond Pass Christian, Mississippi, I stopped and bought some sandwiches and a quart thermos which I had filled with coffee. I pulled into a motel, slept until midnight, and went on. It was three-fifteen A.M. when I came into the outskirts of Carthage.

North of the highway in the west end of town is an area of jerry-built houses and old shacks surrounding the cotton gin and ice plant. I turned left at the city limits, went over two blocks, turned right again, and parked near a weather-beaten frame apartment house. A half dozen other cars stood overnight at the curb in the same block, and this one could stay here a week or more before the police wondered about it, even with the Louisiana license plates. I looked up and down the shadowy street; it was deserted, and all the windows were dark. I slid out, grabbed the suitcase, and walked back the way I'd come, in order to cross the highway before it widened into the well-lighted thoroughfare of Clebourne Street.

When I came out to it I could see two or three cars parked before Fuller's neon sign, six blocks to my left, but nothing was moving anywhere. I hurried across and down the street on the opposite side to the corner of Taylor, turned left, and started toward the center of town, feeling naked and exposed and scared. A dog barked, somewhere inside a house. The street lights suspended over the intersections swayed slightly in the wind, setting up weaving patterns of shadow under the bare limbs of the trees. I looked nervously behind me and down the intersecting streets, watching for Cap Deets on his patrol. My shoes made a grating sound on the sidewalk. Two blocks. Three. I passed the intersection of Mason Street, and midway up the block to my left was the softly glowing sign of the Carthage Funeral Home. I shuddered inside the topcoat, and hurried on. I reached Fulton. It was as empty of life as the rest. All I had to do now was cross it, turn left toward Clebourne, and make the last half block to the alley behind the office. I was in the open, still thirty yards from the mouth of the alley, when I heard the car coming along Taylor Street behind me. I broke into a run. Tires squealed softly as the car began its casual turn into Fulton, its headlights swinging. Just before they reached me, I flung myself into the alley and flattened against the wall behind a utility pole. The car went on past, toward Clebourne; behind the pole, I couldn't tell whether it was a police car or not.

I remained plastered limply against the wall for a moment while I groped in my pocket for the keys and selected the right one. The alley was dark except for the window at the rear of Fuller's kitchen, and there was no sound except the humming of the exhaust fan above it. I strode over, unlocked the door, and breathed softly in relief as it closed behind me. The door into the outer office at the far end was closed, so the passage was in utter darkness, but I needed no light. To my left was the door to the washroom, and just beyond it, on the right, was the side entrance to my office. I groped my way along to it, stepped inside, and closed it.

To my left, a faint crack of light along the floor marked the location of the door opening into the outer office, facing the front windows and the street. Behind my desk, over on the right, was a small window on the alley. I felt my way back to it and checked to be sure the slats of the Venetian blind were closed, but even then I didn't dare turn on a light. The glow of the window would be visible in the alley. I rolled my topcoat into a pillow and lay down on the rug in front of the desk. They'd never think of looking for me here. But everything now depended on Barbara Ryan; if she believed I'd killed Frances, she would call the police.

I awoke to gray dimness inside the room and looked at my watch. It was after seven. Taking the toilet kit from the bag, I went across the passage to the washroom to shave, and brush my teeth. After I'd put on a fresh shirt and brushed some of the lint off my suit, I felt less like the tag end of a four-day drunk and ready to face whatever was going to happen. I ate one of the sandwiches, drank a cup of coffee from the thermos, and sat down in the swivel chair behind the desk with a cigarette. She should be here in about ten minutes; she always opened the office at eight, while Turner and Evans, the two salesmen, came in around a quarter of nine. I wrote out a copy of the telegram I'd given Mac, and waited.

The door to the outer office was in front of me, but off to the left; when it was open, anyone passing on the sidewalk outside could see in, but wouldn't be able to see the desk. I could hear the traffic outside on Clebourne and the rattle of trash cans in the alley as the garbage truck went through. Once in a while, very faintly, there was a clatter of dishes from Fuller's, just on the other side of the wall to my right. I thought of the twenty, or thirty people who were in there now, eating breakfast, and of what they were saying. Mulholland would be there.

The front door had opened. I heard a desk drawer open and close as she stowed away her purse. There were no voices, so she was alone. A minute or two went by, and then I heard the staccato clicking of the typewriter. I reached out a hand toward the button, but hesitated, aware of the suffocation in my chest. What would she do? Scream? Run into the street? Call Scanlon? Well, as Mac would say, shoot or hand somebody else the gun. I pressed the buzzer.

The clicking of the typewriter cut off as if the sound had been chopped through with an axe. For several seconds that seemed like minutes, nothing happened. Then a chair scraped. I heard the tapping of high heels, coming this way. A door opened, but it was the other one, going into the passage. I sighed gently, wondering how I could have associated with this girl for a year without discovering she was a genius. To anybody passing along the sidewalk, she was merely going to the john. I leaned back in the chair with my fingers laced together behind my head and looked at the side door. It opened softly. She was wearing a gabardine skirt and a soft cashmere sweater that'd never had that kind of profile when the cashmeres were wearing it. If there was fear or consternation in back of the cool blue eyes, it didn't show.

"Come in," I said.

She stepped inside and closed the door, standing in front of the racked collection of guns along the left wall. Perhaps she had already answered the question, but I had to ask it anyway. "Do you believe I killed her?"

"No," she said.

I wanted to ask why, but we didn't have much time, and there were more important things. "Probably a minority opinion."

She shook her head. "There's considerably more heat than light at the moment, but not everybody believes it, in spite of the way it looks. I think I'm the only one, though, who knew you were coming back."

"You did?"

"Sure. When I realized you wanted Scanlon to know you took those bonds."

"That's right," I said. "He'd know I couldn't go anywhere without money, nor get any after I was on the run, so I had an idea he'd ask if there were anything negotiable in that safe. Sit down, Barbara."

She took one of the black leather armchairs in front of the desk and crossed her legs. I passed her the cigarettes and held the lighter for her. "How did you get back?" she asked.

"Obviously, I didn't. My car's in New Orleans, and if I'd come on the bus somebody would have seen me get off at the station. You haven't seen me."

"I've been thinking I should cut down on the stuff."

"Even if they catch me here in town and discover I've been hiding out in my own office," I went on, "there's no way you could have known it. You wouldn't have any occasion to come in here. The files and every thing are all out there."

She smiled. "All right, if you insist. And what else is there I don't know?"

"That I was listening in on all phone calls—I mean, if my extension happened to be left accidentally jacked in. And about an hour from now you'll receive a telegram from El Paso you won't understand. Here's a copy of it."

I passed it over. She read it, nibbling thoughtfully at her lower lip. "Umh-umh. It *would* be a little on the murky side, since we don't know any Mr. Weaver and we have no file number W-511. But being an alert and clean-living type of girl who's always right in there polishing the apple and bucking for a raise, I'd probably go ahead and call the Norman Agency, since you're not here to do it."

"Right," I said. "Then when you find out this Norman outfit is a detective agency and that the telegram's from me, you turn the whole thing over to Scanlon, including the information Norman gives you—if any."

She grinned. "Zzzzhhh! What a back-stabbing little priss I am!"

"You're a law-abiding citizen who wouldn't think of withholding information from the police. So later in the day when a couple of other telegrams come in, one from Houston and the other from Miami, you read them over the phone to Scanlon too."

"Yes, I suppose I'm just the type that would. And probably be stupid enough to leave the intercom open so you'd hear me dialing. Now, is that a full catalog of the finer aspects of my character, or is there more?"

"Just one thing. You probably don't know what the feature is today at the Crown Theatre?"

"No, but I have a feeling I'm dying to find out. Let's see— today's Saturday, so the box office'll open at two." Her eyes narrowed thoughtfully. "Doris Bentley? I didn't think of her."

"Ernie said Roberts had gone out with her. And, remember, she used to work for Frances. I've got a hunch there's a connection somewhere."

She nodded. "Could be. Do you think you'd recognize the voice if you heard it again?"

"It's worth a try."

"Do you think she knows something about it?"

"I don't know," I said. I told her just what the girl had said over the phone. "There's another man mixed up in the thing somewhere, and if we find out who he is, we might get somewhere." Then I went on and told her briefly about the money and the fact Norman believed Frances had been tailed by a private detective at least part of the time she was in New Orleans.

She looked up eagerly. "Could we find out who hired him?"

"No, but the police can."

She crossed her fingers. "Good luck. I'd better get back out there."

I stood up. "I don't know how to thank you."

She smiled. "You can't. You're in El Paso." She started to turn away. "Oh, incidentally, the phones will be on the line together, so if we don't want two separate clicks, we've got to pick them up at the same time. How about the middle of the third ring?"

"Right," I said. "Smart girl."

She went out, through the side door into the passage. In a moment the typewriter resumed its clatter. I lit a cigarette and tried to think. There must be some connection between the money Frances had got rid of and Roberts' mysterious source of income that puzzled Ernie. But how could there be? The seven thousand dollars had all disappeared within the past week, while from what Ernie had said, the strange business of Roberts' seeming to have more money than he took in must have been going on for months. Well, there was one thing I could check while I was waiting; all the monthly statements of our joint bank account for the past year were here in the desk where I'd been going through them for items deductible on my income tax return. I softly eased the drawer open, arranged the twelve brown envelopes in order on the desk, and started through them, sorting out and writing down the amounts of all checks she had made out to cash. On another sheet of paper I put down the totals by months. It took about a half hour. I was just finishing when the phone rang.

On the third ring I picked it up, holding my hand over the mouthpiece. "Warren Realty," Barbara said. "Good morning."

It was a woman's voice, charged with venom. "Then it is true! When I heard it, I didn't believe it was possible."

"What do you mean?" Barbara asked.

"*What do I mean*?" She sounded as though she were strangling. "I mean that you're still working for that monster! Or don't you have any sense of decency at all?"

Barbara broke in sweetly, "Oh, has he been convicted? I didn't even know they'd held the trial."

"*Well, of all the loathsome*—!" There was a crash, and the line went dead. I replaced the receiver.

The typewriter resumed its cadence in the outer room. There was a momentary pause, and I heard faint background noise from the intercom at my left elbow. "Charming old biddy," she said, as if she were speaking out of the side of her mouth. "The finance company must have repossessed her broom." The speaker went dead.

I wondered how much of that she'd had to contend with yesterday, and how much there'd be today. I felt guilty, leaving her out there to endure it alone, while I hid. Wrenching my mind away from it, I returned to the column of figures, trying to find some pattern. Roberts had come here and opened his shop in April, but for the first seven months of the year, from January through July, the checks she had written for cash had averaged about $200 per month, ranging from a low of $145 to a high of $315. Then in August the total had jumped to $625, including two for $200 apiece. September was $200 again. October was $365, November $410, and December $500.

It wasn't very conclusive. From the time Roberts had arrived in April, until August, there was no change. Then from August through December she'd cashed checks for a total of $2100, or an average of a little over $400 per month. That would be about $200 above the average for the rest of the year. It might be significant, but it certainly wasn't enough to account for Ernie's story. In a carelessly run business, $200 a month could disappear without a trace.

But still the similarity of the ways they had come here was too much of a coincidence. Had they known each other before? You could concede that one person might come to a small town where he knew no one at all and open a business, a town apparently chosen at random—but two? It was improbable.

I heard the front door open. It was probably Evans or Turner. But when I looked at my watch I saw it was already nine-fifty-five; they probably weren't even going to show up. There was an indistinguishable murmur of voices, and then the door opened again. The intercom came on. "Here we go," she whispered. I snatched eagerly at the telephone. The telegram had come.

CHAPTER 7

SHE DIALED THE OPERATOR AND put through the call. In a moment a girl's voice said, "Norman Detective Agency."

"*Detective* agency?" Barbara asked.

"Yes. Are you sure you have the right number?"

"Well, it must be, if this is the Norman agency. Could I speak to Mr. Norman, please?"

When he came on the line, she said, "This is the Warren Realty Company in Carthage—"

"Who's speaking?" he asked.

"Barbara Ryan. Mr. Warren's not here, and we've received a rather strange telegram from a Mr. Weaver, in—"

He cut her off. "Never mind where it's from; if it's what I think it is, I'd just as soon not know. Maybe you'd better read it to me."

She read it.

"Umh-umh," he said. "Your telegram's from your boss."

"From Mr. Warren *himself*?"

"In person. He pulled a whizzer on me, and now he's about to pull one on you."

"How do you mean?"

"He wants some information I've got for him, but if you pass it along to him without telling the police where he is you're sticking your neck out a mile. When he hired me to get this information for him he didn't tell me he was hotter than radioactive cobalt; I had to find that out by reading the papers last night, like any other dope. And now I'm expecting the cops to come pounding on the door any minute; they know he was here in town, and it was *Mrs.* Warren we asked five thousand people about yesterday. But that's all right; I don't know where he is, and I don't want to know."

"Would you be breaking any law if you gave me the information?"

"No. I've got a signed authorization to do it, as long as you have that file number. What you do with it is your pigeon."

"I suppose, under the circumstances, I should give it to the police, along with the telegram. But if Mr. Warren calls, I'll also give it to him. After all, he's paying for it. You don't object to the police knowing he hired you, do you?"

"No. As long as I'm not withholding information as to his whereabouts, I'm in the clear. I don't think it'll be much help to him, but we have found out what he wanted. I mean, what his wife was doing down here."

I waited tensely. "What was it?" Barbara asked.

"She was playing the ponies."

That trumpet call! I cursed myself for a tone-deaf idiot; anybody else would have placed it long ago. It was the same one they always play at racetracks when the horses come out to parade to the post. She'd called from a booth somewhere near the track.

"Are you sure of that?" Barbara asked.

"No doubt of it at all. For the whole week she was out there every afternoon the track was open. And she really dropped a wad. At four yesterday afternoon we located two taxi drivers who remembered taking her out to the track on different days, so we shagged out there and started flashing her picture to the sellers. We didn't have any luck until we hit the $50 window, but *he* remembered her all right. She'd been throwing it in to the tune of $200 and $300 a race, especially the last couple of days. We also found where she hocked the coat. She got $350 for it, a mink worth three or four thousand. If Warren's lawyer could get enough husbands with bingo-playing wives on the jury, he'd be a cinch to beat it"

"Do you have any other information?"

"Two items. We're certain there wasn't any other man involved. And equally certain somebody was having her tailed, at least part of the time."

"You mean followed? By a private detective?"

"Yes. I told Warren about it yesterday. Later we found out for sure."

"Do you know the agency this detective works for?"

"For himself. He's a kind of fringe-area gumshoe named Paul Denman. That about wraps it up as far as we're concerned. Warren has a balance due him from the money he paid us, and we'll send you a check."

"Thank you very much." She hung up.

I stared hopelessly at the wall. Horses? It was insane. In the eighteen months we'd been married she'd never mentioned horses, and she'd never gambled on anything except bridge at a tenth of a cent a point. But it didn't matter; it obviously had nothing to do with her being killed, and the whole thing had been for nothing. No. There was Denman. When we found out who was having her followed, we might have the answer to everything. Barbara was dialing again.

"Sheriff's office, Scanlon speaking."

"Mr. Scanlon, this is Barbara Ryan. I have something here that perhaps you should know about. I—uh—" She hesitated.

"Yes, what is it?"

"Well; it's a telegram. And it seems to be from Mr. Warren."

"Warren?" he broke in. "Where's it from?"

"El Paso. Texas. But maybe I'd better read it to you." She read it, and went on. "I couldn't make any sense out of it at first, but when I called this Mr. Norman he turned out to be a private detective, and he said the telegram's from Mr. Warren and that legally I'm obliged to turn it over to the police—"

"Good for you, Mrs. Ryan. Hold on a minute." I heard him giving orders to somebody in the room. "Get over to Warren's office and pick up a telegram Mrs. Ryan's got for us. And make it fast." He came back on the line. "Now. What else did this Norman say?"

She repeated the conversation, and asked, "What should I do if Mr. Warren does call?"

"Give him the information, but don't tell him we know anything about it. Keep him on the line as long as you can. We'll alert the telephone company and the El Paso police."

"Well, all right," she agreed reluctantly. "But I still feel like a Judas. He thought he could depend on me."

"Mrs. Ryan, get it through your head—Warren's either the coldest-blooded murderer of this century, or a dangerous maniac in the last stages of paranoia. Take a look at it yourself—ten minutes after he beat his wife to death with an andiron, he was in my office accusing me of persecuting him, and demanding a lawyer to defend his constitutional rights. Personally, I just think he'd forgotten he'd killed her. He even told George Clement he didn't know when she was coming home. And when Owens went out there to see why he didn't answer the phone, he'd been *asleep*. Good God in Heaven—probably in the same room! He's dangerous to himself and to everybody else, as long as he's at large."

"You refuse to consider the possibility he could be innocent?"

He sighed wearily. "Listen. Everybody's innocent until he's proved guilty, even a maniac. And I'm not trying the case, anyway; all I'm trying to do is grab him before he kills somebody else."

"But what about this information from Norman? Or even the fact that Mr. Warren hired him in the first place?"

"To investigate his wife, after he'd already killed her?"

"No, no. I mean the fact that somebody else was having her followed, *before* she was killed. If you could find out who hired tins man Denman—"

There was pity in his voice. "You mean you don't know?"

"He couldn't have."

"God knows how many detectives he's hired. We'll probably hear next he's having me investigated. Or Roberts."

"All right, Mr. Scanlon, if you don't want to look into this, I'm afraid I can't cooperate with you. I'll tell him—"

"Hold it!" he broke in. "Don't get yourself in trouble. Of course I'll check it; that's what I'm here for. I'll ask the New Orleans police to question this Denman, but you know as well as I do it was Warren that hired him."

"I still say the whole thing's a horrible mistake; I know Mrs. Warren was still alive after he left the house with Mulholland."

"It's no good, Mrs. Ryan. You admit yourself you can't place the time nearer than fifteen minutes; it was before he left, when he was bawling me out."

That was puzzling. What the devil were they talking about?

"All right," she said then. "I'll do it."

"Good for you. You've been a lot of help."

"I do think, though, you should let me know what Denman says."

"I will." He hung up.

I heard the deputy come in and pick up the telegram. In the next two hours there were five telephone calls, three of them from newspapers wanting background information, one from a man who identified himself and said he thought I was innocent, and the last from a man who didn't identify himself and said when I was caught and brought back I'd be lynched. She signaled on the intercom when she went out to lunch so I wouldn't pick up the phone. It rang once while she was gone. When she returned, she came on down the passage toward the washroom and pushed open the side door. She slid a chair up close to the desk and sat down.

"What was that about with Scanlon?" I asked.

"I've only got a minute, but that's what I wanted to explain. I tried to call you last night—I mean, night before last—to ask if you'd heard the story going around town that Roberts had been murdered instead of accidentally shooting himself. But the line was busy."

"What time?" I asked quickly.

"That's the trouble. All I'm certain of is that it was right around eleven-forty-five, between there and midnight. They say it was eleven-forty-five when you left the house with Mulholland, and that you'd been on the phone, talking to Scanlon. They think that's what it was. God, if I'd only looked at the clock."

"There's no doubt she called somebody, as soon as I was out the door."

"But why? To get herself killed?"

"I don't know," I said helplessly. "I'm so fouled up now I'm not sure of my own name. Norman's information was no help at all."

"Well, there's still Denman. I wanted to tell you, if necessary you can talk back on the intercom. Evans and Turner aren't here, and nobody can hear you from the street. I'm facing the other way, so they can't see my lips move. If somebody comes in, I'll cut the switch."

"Good girl. You're wonderful."

She grinned sardonically. "I guess I'm a born cloak-and-dagger type. But it's almost one; I'm going to call Doris Bentley."

She went out. I picked up the phone and waited tensely while she dialed.

"Crown Theatre."

"Would you tell me what the feature is today, please?" Barbara asked.

"Yes. It's Gregory Peck in 'The Bravados.'" My pulse leaped; I was certain it was the right voice.

"And what time does it start, please?"

"At one-thirty-five, just after the news and the cartoon."

"Thank you."

Barbara hung up, and in a moment the intercom hummed. "What do you think?" she asked softly.

I pressed the key and leaned close to the box. "She's the girl; I'm sure of it."

"What now?"

"I'm going to talk to her."

"How can you?"

"We'll wait till the picture starts and she's not busy. Can you do an imitation of a long-lines operator?"

"Sure. But, listen—if she reports it to Scanlon, he'll know it's a fake. The phone company's watching all incoming calls."

"I don't think she'll report it, for the same reason she's never identified herself. She's not eager for publicity."

"Here's hoping."

I waited nervously while a half hour dragged by. The chances were she'd refuse to admit she was the one unless I could scare her. She obviously didn't want to be identified, either because she was mixed up in this thing herself, or from a natural disinclination to admit she'd been in Roberts' apartment—which was the only way she could have found the lighter there. The intercom came on, and I heard Barbara dialing.

"Crown Theatre."

"This is long-distance. We have call for a Miss Doris Bentley. Is she there?"

"Long distance?"

"Yes. El Paso is calling. For Miss Bentley."

"This is Miss Bentley, but—"

"Go ahead, please."

"Hello," I said. "Hello, Doris?" I heard her gasp. "It took me a long time to remember where I'd heard your voice before."

"Who are you?" she demanded. "And what are you talking about?"

"You know who I am, so let's get down to cases. And don't hang up on me, because if you do Scanlon's going to pick you up. I've still got a friend or two there, and he might get a tip; you didn't invent the anonymous telephone call."

"Just a moment, please," she said sweetly. I heard her put down the phone, and then the rattle of coins from the change dispenser.

She came back. "You wouldn't dare! I'd tell him where you are."

"Try me and see. After all, they're going to catch me sooner or later, so I haven't got much to lose. But you have, haven't you?"

"What is it you want?"

"The name of the other man."

"What other man?"

"*Listen*—when you called me, you said Roberts wasn't the only one. What's his name?"

"I don't know."

"All right. You're asking for it."

"I tell you, I don't know. All I know is there was one. It was when I was still working for her, before she married."

"How do you know there was?"

"I just do," she said sullenly.

"I said *how*?"

"I've got eyes, haven't I? The stuck-up witch, she didn't fool me—"

"You really hated her, didn't you?"

"So what if I did?"

"Why?"

"That's my business. And, anyway, she was the one got Roberts killed, wasn't she?"

"I don't know. That's what I'm trying to find out"

"Now, there's a hot one. That's a real gas."

"Did you ever tell Roberts about this man?"

"No."

"Because he didn't exist, isn't that right?"

"All right, you have it your way. I still know what I know."

"Did Roberts ever ask you anything about her?"

"No. Except once, I think he did ask me what her name was before she was married. And where she came from."

"Did he say why he asked?"

"No."

"When was this?"

"It was way last summer."

"Do you remember exactly?"

"Why are you asking all these stupid questions? I think it was the first time we dated. In July, or June—I don't know. Stop bothering me. I don't want to talk about it anymore." The line went dead.

The intercom came on, and Barbara asked, "What do you make of it?"

"Not much. Maybe she's lying about the other man."

"I'm not too sure; though she *is* bitter about something. It might be Roberts' death, of course. But there's still something odd about the way she held out on that one point—I mean, how she knew there was somebody else."

"And still doesn't know who he is. Or says she doesn't."

"Or who he *was*. I just remembered something while you were talking. Didn't she used to date Junior Delevan?"

I frowned. "Yes. Now I think of it, she did."

"I don't know what that could have to do with this, but she does have bad luck with her boyfriends." The speaker went silent.

Delevan was a wild, good-looking kid with a penchant for trouble; he'd been arrested several times for car theft while still in high school, and later had been convicted of burglary and given a suspended sentence. Then just about two years ago they'd found his body on the city dump one morning with the top of his head broken in. The police never found out who'd done it.

As I recalled now, it was just before Frances and I were married, while she was still running the shop, but she couldn't have had anything to do with him. She was twenty-five then, and he couldn't have been over nineteen. She probably didn't even know him, except she might have seen him with Doris a time or two.

The intercom hummed. "Telegram," she whispered. I grabbed the phone just as she started to dial.

"Sheriff's office, Mulholland."

"Could I speak to Mr. Scanlon, please? This is Mrs. Ryan."

"I think it could be arranged, honey; but wouldn't I do?" You could see the smirk on the stupid bastard's face. I wondered how it would look with a boot sticking out of it.

"If you don't mind," she said coolly, "I'd rather speak to Mr. Scanlon."

"Right you are, sweetie."

When Scanlon came on the line, she said, "This is Barbara Ryan again. I've just received another telegram—"

"From Warren?" he broke in.

"No. It's from Houston, Texas, and it is addressed *to* Mr. Warren. The text reads as follows: DAN ROBERTS BORN HOUSTON 1933, ORPHANED AT AGE TWELVE, RAISED BY OLDER BROTHER CLINTON ROBERTS OWNER DOWNTOWN SPORTING GOODS STORE STOP JOINED HOUSTON POLICE FORCE 1954 BECAME DETECTIVE VICE SQUAD 1957 SUSPENDED AND INDICTED FOR EXTORTION 1958 STOP DREW SUSPENDED SENTENCE STOP APRIL LAST YEAR BROTHER ADVANCED MONEY ESTABLISH HIMSELF IN BUSINESS ELSEWHERE GET NEW START AWAY FROM ASSOCIATIONS HERE STOP HAS NEVER BEEN IN FLORIDA UNLESS SINCE LAST APRIL STOP NO DANGEROUS ENEMIES BUT WITH KIND OF FRIENDS HE HAD HE DIDN'T NEED ANY SIGNED CATES."

"What do you suppose it means?" Barbara asked then.

"I don't know," Scanlon replied wearily. "But I'm getting afraid to open my desk drawer for a cigar; a couple of Warren's detectives might jump out in my face. We just heard from New Orleans."

"About Denman?"

"Yes. He says he was hired by a man from here by the name of Joseph Randall."

"Randall? I don't think I know anybody—"

"Exactly."

"But didn't he meet this Randall? Or doesn't he have an address, or phone number?"

"No. Randall called him by long-distance and hired him to follow Mrs. Warren. Said he'd send him the retainer, which he did—in cash, through the mail. That was Monday. He called Denman Tuesday night and then again Wednesday night, for his report. We're having the phone company check out the calls now, but they'll turn out to be from a pay phone. It's so damn characteristic of paranoia—you've got to be sly, and fool 'em; everybody's plotting against you."

"But it could have been somebody else. Naturally, he'd want to keep his identity secret—"

He sighed. "Mrs. Ryan, did you ever hear of anybody hiring a detective to watch another man's wife?"

"Then why would Denman take the assignment under those circumstances?"

"He has the reputation of not being too fussy about who hires him as long as he gets paid."

The last lead was gone now. I slumped over the desk with my head in my hands. I'd have been better off if I'd given myself up in the first place. Heels tapped in the passage, and the door opened softly. Barbara had her purse under her arm.

She smiled. "A girl's entitled to rebuild her face before the coffee break." Seating herself by the desk, she slid a yellow envelope from the purse. "This just came, and I don't think I've got the nerve to read him another one this soon."

"Thanks." I dropped in the chair behind the desk and tore it open.

JOHN D. WARREN
WARREN REALTY
CARTHAGE ALABAMA:

NO SUCH PERSON AS FRANCES KINNAN STOP HAVE CHECKED VITAL STATISTICS ORLANDO AND DADE COUNTY NO BIRTH NO MARRIAGE NO DIVORCE STOP UNHEARD OF AT UNIVERSITY OF MIAMI AND BURDINES STOP NO RECORD OF A LEON DUPRE NOR SHOP ANYWHERE MIAMI AREA NAMED LEONS STOP ADVISE FURTHER ACTION DESIRED

CROSBY INVESTIGATIONS

I read it, and silently passed it to her.

CHAPTER 8

SHE READ IT.

"Any ideas?" she asked at last.

"One," I said. "Quit, while I still know who *I* am."

"Maybe it's not quite as hopeless as that," she replied. "It seems to me you've pretty well established what was at the bottom of it. You have a man with a previous record of extortion, and a woman—" She hesitated, embarrassed.

"It's all right," I said. "We've got no time to search for euphemisms; let's call 'em as they fall. A woman with something to hide, possibly a criminal record. Result: blackmail. But it still makes no sense." I showed her the figures from the bank statements. "I'll admit the pattern matches what Doris Bentley said—that Roberts first asked about her along in the summer. For the sake of argument we'll assume he had some reason to suspect she wasn't who she'd said she was. Then maybe he started checking, and found out what she was trying to cover up. So far, so good—it was in August the checks she wrote for cash suddenly took a jump. But look at the picayune amounts: $200 a month at most. And all the time she had $6000 of her own she didn't touch—until this week when she threw it away on a bunch of glue-footed horses. That doesn't sound very desperate to me.

And, finally, she didn't kill Roberts, anyway; she wasn't even in the same state."

"No," she said. "But aren't you overlooking the possibility two people could have been paying blackmail? If Doris is right, she had a boyfriend."

I looked at her thoughtfully. "Maybe you've got it! And that would account for Roberts' income that Ernie couldn't figure out. There's no telling how much he was tapping this other party for."

"It's about the only thing that fits the facts we have now," she said.

I lit a cigarette, and one for her. "There's one more thing that puzzles me at the moment," I said. "How did you ever work for me for a full year without my finding out you had more sense than I have?"

She gave me that cynical, lopsided grin. "Hiding that from the boss is the first thing any secretary learns." She went on, "Seriously, though—"

"Seriously, though," I interrupted her, "I'm beginning to think the only smart thing I've done in years was hire you, when you left George. Incidentally, why did you quit him? I don't think you ever told me."

She shrugged. "I just didn't like legal work, I guess. It's too fussy—ten copies of everything, and no erasures. But let's get back to the brainstorming. The next question telegraphs itself."

"Right," I said. "What was the boyfriend so afraid of, that he'd pay off to Roberts? Scandal? Divorce?"

She shook her head. "It must have been more than that. He not only paid off, he finally killed him. And her, too."

I nodded. "I still think Doris Bentley knows more about it than she'll admit. Do you suppose it *could* have had something to do with Junior Delevan? She was still working for Frances then."

She nibbled at her lower lip. "Yes, I think she was. I've been trying to remember exactly when it happened. In May, wasn't it, two years ago? It was Sunday morning when they found his body, and the medical examiner estimated he'd been killed around midnight the night before."

"Sure, I remember now. I was in Tampa on business and didn't hear about it until I got back, the following Tuesday, I think—" I paused, trying to recall something. "Wait a minute! I've got it now. I had a date with Frances that Saturday night, to take her to a country club dance at Rutherford, but had to break it at the last minute and drive to Mobile to catch a plane. And now that I think about it, she was acting a little strangely when I came back, as if something were bothering her. I just thought it was because of the broken date."

"Well, she couldn't have killed Junior—not without an elephant gun. Or carried his body out there to the dump. He was a pretty big boy—around 200 pounds."

A wild idea was beginning to nudge the edge of my mind. It was a forlorn hope, but all I had now. "I've got to talk to Doris. If she knows anything, I'll scare it out of her."

She stared at me. "You can't leave here."

"I can't stay here forever, either. None of this has got me anywhere; I started out trying to find out who'd killed Frances, and now I don't even know who she was. I'm just going backward."

"Somebody'll see you. Or she'll call the police."

"I'll have to risk it. Do you know where she lives?"

She still looked scared. "No. But if you insist, I can find out. And I'll drive you."

"No. Absolutely not."

She stood up. "I've got to get back out front. I'll talk to you later."

She called Scanlon and read him the telegram from Crosby.

"What do you think now?" she asked.

"That I must be crazy myself: I asked for this job."

"Don't you consider that this information changes the picture a little?"

"Nothing can change the facts, Mrs. Ryan. Warren killed her, no matter who she was."

"I thought you weren't trying the case, Mr. Scanlon."

He sighed. "I'm not. But Warren was there in the house alone when she drove the car into the garage, and when he left the house she was dead. There's no way anybody can climb out of that. It's sealed, it's final. But never mind that. Just remember, when he calls, all you have to do is keep him talking as long as possible. The telephone company and the El Paso Police will do the rest And he should call any time now."

"All right," she said, her tone edged with bitterness. "But if it develops there's a reward for the job, don't forget to send it to me in silver."

"Stop beating yourself over the head. Do you want him to kill somebody else before we can catch him?"

She went out after awhile for coffee, and when she came back there was somebody with her. I could hear a man's voice I thought was Turner's; apparently he'd decided to come in for something. The typewriter clattered. At five-thirty I heard them preparing to leave. Her heels clicked down the passage as she went to the washroom, and a folded sheet of paper slid under the door. I picked up the typed message.

"Doris Bentley lives in that apartment house at the corner of Taylor and Westbury. Apartment 2C. This is Saturday, so she'll probably have a date after she gets off work. I'll find out and let you know. Since you can't answer the phone unless you're sure it's me, let it ring at least ten times.

"Questions, pertinent and impertinent: If F. were hiding from something or somebody, why did she choose Carthage? Just at random? Was that apartment at the rear of the store furnished as living quarters at the time she rented it? And was that space the best available in town at the time for a dress shop? Assuming Doris is right about the boyfriend, how did the two of them get by with it in a town this size without anybody but Doris ever suspecting?"

Smart girl, I thought; you're priceless. I lit a cigarette and sat frowning at the sheet of paper. The implication was clear, and along the same line as the thought I'd already had—that it was improbable that *two* people would come to a town where they knew no one at all and open businesses. My idea, of course, had been that she and Roberts had known each other somewhere before; on the information I had now, that seemed very unlikely. And after all, she'd come here over a year before Roberts had. So maybe she knew somebody else, who was already here. Who'd brought her here. And was it because of the apartment? Or rather, its location? I tried to remember the places available at the time. There'd been a vacant store in this block, I was pretty sure, which would have been a better location for that type shop. Of course, I'd given her a good sales talk, but she hadn't been hard to convince.

It wasn't much of an apartment, just a small pullman kitchen, bathroom, and combined living room and bedroom, but it was already completely furnished. There were two entrances, one through the front of the store, and the other on the alley—or rather, into the vestibule at the foot of the rear stairs coming down from the second floor.

I began to feel the proddings of excitement. Naturally, a man going in and out the front door of a main street dress shop, open or closed, day or night, would be as conspicuous as a broken leg in a chorus line, and the rear entrance wasn't a great deal better. But suppose he was already in the building, a tenant of one of the offices on the second floor? Then the excitement drained away as I named them over in my mind: Dr. Martin; George Clement; Dr. Atlee; Dr. Sawyer, the dentist. Sawyer and Martin were both at least 65, Dr. Atlee was a woman, and George—it was ridiculous.

But the idea refused to die altogether. George and Dr. Martin were both members of the Duck Club. And pillars of the community had been caught off base before, plenty of times. Then I grunted, and ground out the cigarette. The whole thing was pure speculation, and where was there any motive for murder, anyway? The man I was looking for had killed two people; he'd been afraid of something worse than a divorce and a little scandal.

The room began to grow dark, but I didn't dare turn on a light. I wondered if I could stand another six or seven hours alone with my thoughts without going mad. I wished Barbara would call. At last I could stand it no longer, and called her, holding the cigarette lighter so I could see to dial. Her line was busy. I waited five minutes and was about to try again when the phone began to ring. I let it ring ten times and picked it up.

"Hello," she said softly. "I've just been talking to Paul Denman in New Orleans."

"Did you learn anything?"

"Very little, and nothing that's any help. He doesn't remember much about this Randall's voice except that it was in the low baritone range and the man sounded as if he were reasonably well educated. Could be any one of a dozen men here in town—including you. He says it *might* be possible he'd recognize the voice if he heard it again, but he'd never be able to pick it out of a number of others in the same register, and as far as evidence is concerned it would be useless in court. The money Randall sent him was in a plain white envelope you can buy in any dime store. Typewriter addressed. No message with it."

"Looks like a dead end there," I said. "But thanks a million for trying."

"I'm going out now to see what Doris Bentley does when she gets off work, and I'll call you later."

I waited. I began thinking about Frances, and seeing the ruin of her face before me in the dark, and knew I had to stop it or I'd go crazy. I tried to force my thoughts back into some logical approach to the solution of the thing, but my mind was numb. I'd been struggling with it too long. Then I found myself thinking of Barbara, and of the old cliché that you never know who your friends are until you're in trouble.

She was originally from Rutherford, and had had the misfortune to fall in love with and marry a kid whose life was all behind him by the time he could vote. Johnnie Ryan at 18 was like Alexander at 32 or whatever it was. Rutherford is a town that's as football-crazy as Texas, to begin with, and Ryan was the greatest halfback the high school had ever produced. Most kids take it in stride, but apparently those autumn afternoons of jampacked stands all screaming, "Oh, Johnnie, oh, Johnnie, how you can run!"—with probably too many of the girls having good reason to remember the original words of the song—had done something to him from which he could never recover. He'd gone off to Ole Miss on an athletic scholarship, but he was up against tougher competition there and never quite made it back to the pinnacle. He tried out with the Chicago Bears the autumn he and Barbara were married, but discovered that high school clippings didn't buy you anything in a pro outfit where they played football for keeps, and he'd come home after a month.

She'd never talked about it, but I guess it was pretty rough being married to an ex-hero. He'd done all right for a while, selling cars in Rutherford, and then in New Orleans, and Mobile, and Oxford, Mississippi, and finally here in Carthage, working for Jim MacBride, but the commissions were growing smaller as the drunks got bigger and longer and the extra-marital affairs more numerous. Maybe it was simply a matter of needing new and adoring faces and the haze of alcohol to bring back the old feeling of greatness, because there was nothing mean or vicious about him and he was generally well-liked. But in the end there were just too many girls, apparently. When he'd moved on—to Florida, I think—Barbara had stayed. Six years of it was enough. She already had a job as a stenographer at the Southland Tide Company and a Notary's commission. George handled the divorce for her, and had offered her a job in his office at more money, so she'd gone to work for him in the fall of 1958. But after less than a year she'd resigned and had come to work for me. That was a year ago last September.

The hours dragged by. It was eleven-thirty. Midnight. I began to tense up. It was going to be dangerous, but anything was better than staying here. The phone rang shortly after one A.M.

"Doris has a date, all right. With Mulholland."

I came instantly alert. "What do you suppose that means?"

"Could be anything. Or nothing except that he's 25 and single, she's pretty, and it's Saturday night. It's pretty hard to stamp out that sort of thing."

"Well, you're having a fine Saturday night," I said regretfully. "Did you break a date to do all this?"

"No, I didn't have one. I seem to be at an awkward age; too old for football rallies and too young for bingo. They're out at the Neon Castle, dancing."

The Neon Castle—the real name of it was Castleman's Inn—was a roadside restaurant and night club about ten miles east of town. "I followed them out there," she said, "to be sure that was where they were headed. Even if they only stay a couple of hours, they'll have to park somewhere afterward for the Machine Age fertility ritual, so it'll probably be three or later before she gets home. In the meantime I've been busy with my do-it-yourself detective kit, and I've got a couple of ideas I want to talk over with you. I'll pick you up in my car—"

"No," I said. "I won't let you take the chance—"

She cut me off. "Don't argue, Duke. You'd never get to her apartment afoot; there are still a few people on the streets. In five minutes I'll be parked at the mouth of the alley. When you come out the back door, stay against the wall and watch me. If the street's clear, I'll signal. Get in back and crouch down."

I opened my mouth to protest, but she'd hung up.

I checked my watch with the aid of the cigarette lighter, groped around for the topcoat, and put it on. When five minutes had passed, I slipped out into the passage, and pushed open the back door. The alley was in deep shadow, and silent except for the humming of Fuller's exhaust fan. Her Ford pulled up and stopped at the curb just beyond the mouth of it, and I could see her rather dimly in the light from the street lamp at the intersection of Clebourne. She motioned, and opened the rear door. I crossed the sidewalk on the run, dived in, and knelt on the floor between the seats.

"All clear," she whispered. "There was nobody in sight." The car was in motion then, and turned right, east along Clebourne. I kept my head down, but could see the blinking amber light as we passed the first street intersection. She turned left at the next one. We were going north on Montrose. I heard a car pass, going the other way. In a few minutes we turned left again, and appeared to be climbing, and I heard gravel under the tires. We made another sharp left turn, went on a few yards very slowly, and stopped. She cut the engine and I heard the click as she switched off the headlights. "Okay, Duke," she said softly.

I sat up. The car was parked on the brow of the hill just back of the city limits on the north side of town. Behind us and on the left were dark lines of trees, but it was open in front, where the hill started to drop away, and I could see the lighted artery of Clebourne stretching away below us from right to left, from one end of town to the other. We were completely alone up here. The wind had stopped, but there was the sharp bite of frost in the air, and when I opened the door and got out the sky was aflame with the cold glitter of stars. I stood for a moment beside the car, looking out over the town where I was born and where I'd lived most of my life, but all I could think of was the back room of the Carthage Funeral Home where the two of them lay with their shattered and unrecognizable faces on individual white enamel tabletops, and the fact that somewhere in that cluster of lights was the man who had killed them. Asleep, maybe? Or could he sleep? And what was it like just at the moment of waking? I tried to shake off these morbid reflections and get back to a more practical view of the matter; there was more than that down there. There were men who were going to arrest me for murder if they could get their hands on me. I opened the front door and slid in on the seat beside Barbara. She moved over some parcels to make room for me.

"Here," she said, picking up one of the things lying on the seat. It was a pint bottle of whiskey.

"You're an angel," I said.

"No, a St. Bernard, but I get tired of that little cask around my neck. When you've had a drink of that, there's some food."

I took a big drink—straight out of the bottle when she said she didn't want any—felt it unfold inside me, and opened the cardboard box. It contained a steak sandwich, wrapped in three or four big paper napkins and still warm. I tore into it, suddenly realizing I hadn't had anything to eat except a couple of those plywood sandwiches in over 48 hours. When I'd finished it, she uncapped a pint thermos bottle of coffee and poured me a cup.

"Where are the dancing girls, and my Turkish water pipe?" I asked. She grinned, the slender face just visible in the starlight, and dug cigarettes out of her purse. I held the lighter for her, and then lit my own. She was wearing a rough tweed skirt and a sweater, and a cloth coat with the collar turned up under the cascade of reddish brown hair.

"Now," she said, "as they say on Madison Avenue, let's kick this thing around and see what we stub our toe on."

"Right. But first let me say that if I ever get out of this mess, the first thing I'm going to do is petition the court to have you adopt me." I repeated the whole story of night before last, beginning with the anonymous telephone call.

When I'd finished, she nodded, and said, "Maybe you could use a guardian, with that hot-headed approach to everything. But let's break it down. First, Mulholland could have known she was home. If he saw the gloves, he should have realized that was her suitcase. And he left the courthouse while you were still there?"

"Yes. Probably an hour before George and I left."

"But on the other hand, it's almost certain she called somebody the minute you left the house. That's why the line was busy when I tried to call you, because I'm positive it was after eleven-forty-five. So it could have been anybody. Now, remember carefully—how long do you think it was from the time you called George Clement until he arrived in the Sheriff's office?"

"Not over ten minutes," I said, and then did a delayed take. "*George?*"

"Why not?" she asked. "That's the way the police operate, from all the mysteries I've read. Anybody's under suspicion until he's been cleared by the facts. Also, there's something else I'll get to shortly—a couple of things—but first let's look at that ten minutes. How many blocks would he have to drive to go from his to your house and then to the courthouse?"

I ran it in my mind, beginning at his house in the east end of town. Three west on Clebourne, five south on Montrose, five back, three more west on Clebourne, and two north on Stanley. "Eighteen. It's impossible. Also, he had to dress."

"He *said* he had to dress. But suppose he was already dressed and on his way out, because of another telephone call he'd received a few minutes before?"

I turned. "By God—!"

"And unless time was a factor—that is, to him—why would he even mention it? It's not in character. Clement has a brilliant and incisive mind, the type that seldom wastes time on trivia."

"But, still—Ten minutes? It's not enough."

She went on. "There would have been little or no traffic at that time of night. We'll clock it, under the same conditions, and see. That's one of the things I picked you up for."

"But wait a minute," I broke in, as the absurdity of it began to dawn on me. "This is George Clement we're talking about, the ex-mayor, the leading citizen; he's so proper and law-abiding he's a little stuffy sometimes. Also, he's a friend of mine—and of hers— we played bridge together an average of once a week."

"Yes, I know," she said calmly.

"And, listen—I don't think anybody on earth could have walked away from the horror in that bedroom and then, in less than three or four minutes at the outside, into another room where there were people, without its showing on his face. Something would have twitched, or there'd have been no color—except green. Hell, he even called me Hotspur, because I was blowing my stack all over the place. Could anybody face the husband of the woman he'd just beaten to death with an andiron—?"

"He could have," she said. "Remember, I worked for him for almost a year, and women study men a lot more than men are ever aware of. George Clement has the most, perfect—I'd say absolute—control of his features of anybody I've ever seen. I don't say he has that much control over his emotions—in fact, I know he hasn't—but nothing inside shows through when he doesn't want it to. It's like pulling a blind. I've watched him in court when he was in trouble with a hostile witness and an unfriendly judge, and one time I hit him—"

"You *what*?"

She grinned. "All right, so I've been known to give way to a hot-headed impulse myself.".

"But—but—what did you hit him for?"

"Well, it was a little ridiculous, actually, but at the moment that seemed the simplest way to get his hand out of my bra."

"You can't mean—not George?"

"I assure you, George has hands."

I goggled at her. "Well, I'll be damned; the sanctimonious old bastard. So that's the reason you quit?"

"Yes. Not then, but later. He apologized for it, and I thought we understood each other, but all he did was change his approach. I finally got tired of knocking down passes, oblique or otherwise, and resigned. Naturally, I didn't say anything about it when you asked, and wouldn't now except that it has a bearing on this matter. In fact, I would say it was quite relevant. But we were talking about his ability to control his expression. Most men under the circumstances would have been angry and blustered it out, or looked sheepish, or tried to laugh their way out of it, or shown some expression. All he did was pull that blind in back of his face. Imagine, the red splotch on the side of it still showing, where I'd hit him, and he was as calm and poised as if he'd merely offered me a cigarette. 'My apologies, Mrs. Ryan.' He must have been raging inside—at me, and at himself for getting into a ridiculous position—but he went right on dictating without missing a comma."

I was still having trouble assimilating it. "That changes the picture considerably. George *could* be the man we're looking for."

"Of course. Now, there's one other item. Are you sure that Frances Kinnan came here from Florida?"

"Yes. There's no doubt of it. Regardless of the fact that Crosby couldn't pick up her trail down there, she came here from Miami. Her car had Dade County license plates, and she paid the first month's rent on the store with a check on a Miami bank. She was lying about all the rest of it, but she'd been there, and she'd been using the name Frances Kinnan. She had to, because that was the name on the pink slip of the car. I sold it for her when we were married, and bought her that Mercedes."

"You don't recall the date on the slip? I mean, when she bought the car?"

"No. I didn't even look at it. But why?"

"As I recall, she arrived here in January, 1959. Is that right?"

"Yes. It was two years ago this week."

"Well, George had just come back from a Florida fishing trip, less than three weeks before."

"What? Are you sure of that?"

"Positive. I've been thinking back very carefully, to make certain of it. I started work for him in November, 1958, and it was less than a month afterward. There were continuations on a couple of cases he had pending, and he got away for about a week, sometime after the middle of December. He came back just a few days before Christmas. And he was down there alone."

CHAPTER 9

"BY GOD, I THINK YOU'VE got it!" I said. "So that was what those fishing trips were for? He always went alone; Fleurelle didn't care for fishing—or for Florida, either."

"Yes, I know," she said simply. "I've been briefed on what Fleurelle didn't like."

"So you had the frigid wife bit thrown at you too?"

She nodded. "But it's not important now. The thing that is, however, is the fact he could have met Frances Kinnan that trip—" She broke off, making a little grimace of distaste. "I don't like this sort of thing."

"Neither do I," I said. "But it can't be helped. So he met her, only this time he brought the girl home with him. And cooked up that dress shop deal to cover it. He knew about the living quarters in back of the store, and knew the place was vacant—it had been for a couple of months, in fact—" I stopped, realizing we still didn't know the answer.

"What is it?" she asked.

"We're as far in left field as ever. There's no motive for murder in any of this. Take a look. Suppose Roberts did find out something about her—I mean, who she was—and she was paying him to keep it hushed up; it was still nothing to George.

By that time she was married to me. She'd have been in a jam, and *my* face might have been a little red if it suddenly developed the police were looking for my wife because she'd absconded with the assets of some bank in Groundloop, Arizona, but they couldn't pin anything on George, even if the details of this dress shop setup ever came out. He's too shrewd a lawyer to get tagged with a charge of harboring a fugitive—he'd probably thought that all out in advance. He'd simply say he had no idea she was a fugitive, and even if she said otherwise, it'd only be her word against his. Admittedly, the scandal wouldn't have helped his position much here in town, but anybody with George's mind and legal training wouldn't have much trouble weighing the risks of first-degree murder against a minor thing like that and coming up with the safe answer, even if he had no scruples against murder aside from the risk. Let Roberts talk, and be damned to him. And, finally, it's doubtful Roberts even knew there was any connection between her and George. As far as Fleurelle is concerned, she might have divorced him if it all came out, but from my viewpoint that'd hardly qualify as a total disaster."

"I know," she said. "There has to be more to it than we've discovered."

"Also, I still don't think George could have killed her. There simply wasn't enough time between my calling him and his showing up in the Sheriff's office."

"That we can check," she said. "And we will in just a minute. But right now, let's look at that Junior Delevan possibility again. I still have a feeling he fits into it somewhere; you can call it feminine intuition if you want, but there's something very significant in that bitterness of Doris Bentley's toward Frances. At first, I thought it might be because she believed you'd killed Roberts and of course blamed Frances for the fact. She probably still thinks you killed him, but I don't think that's what's bothering her. She didn't care that much about him. They dated a few times, but from what I can find out, that's about all it amounted to. So we have to go back further. She was pretty crazy about Junior, from all accounts.

"I've been asking a few questions here and there, trying not to be too obvious about it, and I've learned just about all that was ever known or ever found out about what happened to Junior that night. And it's not very much. Scanlon questioned Doris about him, along with a lot of other people, but she swears she never saw him at all. She had a date with him, but he stood her up."

Something nebulous brushed against the perimeter of my mind. I tried to close in on it, but it got away. I must have grunted, because she stopped. "What?"

"Sorry," I said. "I was just trying to remember something. Go on."

"She could have been lying about not seeing him," she went on, "but apparently Scanlon was satisfied she was telling the truth. It seems she even called Junior's house, when he failed to show up for the date when the dress shop closed at nine P.M., trying to find out if his mother knew where he was. She—that is, Mrs. Delevan—verified this. She said Doris called there twice. There's not much more to tell. They do know where Junior was until around eleven-thirty. He was with two other boys—Kenny Dowling and Chuck McKinstry—just riding around drinking beer. Dowling was old enough to buy it, so he was picking it up by the six-pack, and they were drinking it in the car. They told Scanlon he got out of the car on Clebourne, near Fuller's, around eleven-thirty, saying he had important business to take care of and couldn't spend the whole night with peasants. They thought he meant a girl, since he always swaggered a bit over his conquests, but he wouldn't tell them her name. They swear that was the last they ever saw of him. Scanlon had them in his office for six hours—he had Dowling where the hair was short, anyway, for giving beer to minors—and when they came out they were pretty sick-looking boys, but they stuck to their story and said they had no idea where he was going or what he was going to do after he left them. Apparently that was the last time he was ever seen alive; he must have been killed in the next half hour. Somewhere."

"Well, our only chance is that Doris knows something about it she hasn't told. Shall we go?"

"Right. But first we time that route."

I got in the back again, crouched down between the seats, with a pencil flashlight she took from her purse. She drove back into the edge of town, turned left, ran two or three blocks, turned right, and stopped. "We're parked on Stuart," she called softly over her shoulder. Stuart was the next cross street east of Clement's big house on Clebourne. "Headed toward Clebourne, a half block from the corner. Starting from here would about equal the time it'd take him to back his car out of the garage. Ready?"

I cupped the little light in my hand and focused it on the watch. When the sweep second hand came around to the even minute, I said, "Take it away."

She pulled away from the curb, and turned right at the corner. A car passed, headed in the opposite direction. I kept down. She turned again, left this time. We were on Montrose. She didn't appear to be driving fast at all. After a moment, she turned right, and then right again. "I'm going around behind," she said quietly. "I doubt he would have parked in your driveway." Probably not, I thought. There were two houses across the street from ours, and he could have been seen. "I'll park at that vacant lot directly behind your house." We eased to the curb and stopped. "Mark."

I flashed the pencil light on the watch, and couldn't believe it at first. "One minute, twelve seconds," I whispered. "It doesn't seem possible."

"I didn't go above 30 miles an hour at any time. All right, here we go for the second leg."

I checked the time as we pulled away. There was very little sound of traffic, even when we turned into Clebourne. In a moment we turned again, went on a short distance, and stopped. "Mark," she said. "We're parked right in front of the courthouse."

I flicked the light on the watch. "One minute and thirty-two seconds. That makes a total of—" I added it quickly. "A total of two minutes forty-four seconds."

"I thought so," she whispered. "You see, he had better than seven minutes. It wouldn't have taken him over two at the most to walk around to the front of your house and then back to the car. He had all the time he needed."

Then—if it *were* George—there'd been no argument, nothing. He must have gone there simply for the purpose of killing her, for cold-blooded, premeditated murder. She'd called him, let him in the house when he rang, and then—the first instant her back was turned—he grabbed up the andiron and brought it down on her head. Why? I shook my head wearily, wondering if anybody would ever know. We started up again.

I could see the blinking amber light at the intersection as we crossed Clebourne. She turned left into Taylor. Westbury was in the east end of town, just beyond the edge of the business district. In a moment we stopped. "Nobody in sight," she whispered.

I sat up. We were at the curb in the middle of the block, in shadow under some trees. All the houses were dark, and there were cars parked ahead and behind us. Up at the next corner, at the street light, was the apartment house. We could see the entrance from here. I checked my watch. It was five minutes of three. "She may be already home," I said.

"Yes, but we don't know where Mulholland is. He might have gone in with her. If they don't show up in half an hour, I'll drive back to the apartment and ring his number to see if I get an answer."

We smoked a cigarette. Fifteen minutes went by in silence as we watched the shadowy, deserted street and the empty pool of light at the corner. The night seemed to have been going on forever, and I wondered where I'd be when it ended. In jail? Or dead? They'd take no chances; if I made a stupid move they'd shoot me.

Doris had had a date with Junior, but he hadn't shown up. Something in that had rung a bell in my mind, very faintly, but I hadn't been able to isolate what it was. She'd tried to get hold of him; she'd called his house—called it twice, in fact. Was she merely incensed because he'd stood her up, or was it something else, something she had to tell him? Just then, a car turned into Taylor two blocks behind us, its headlights flashing briefly in the rear-view mirror.

"Duck," I whispered. We lay down on the seats.

The car came on and went past us. We sat up again. It wasn't a police car, but it was slowing. It went on across the intersection ahead and pulled to the curb before the apartment house entrance. A man got out from the driver's side and went around and opened the other door, a big man, bareheaded. I felt excitement run along my nerves, and began to tense up. It was Mulholland. He helped Doris out, and they crossed the sidewalk to the doorway. I watched nervously to see if he were going to follow her in. He didn't. For a moment the two figures blended as they kissed, and then she went inside and he came back to the car. He drove on down Taylor and turned left at the next corner.

"Give him five minutes, to be sure he doesn't come back," she said softly. "And, remember—try not to scare her too much. If she panics, she'll scream. I'll drop you off right in front, and then go on and park in the next block."

"No," I whispered. "If anybody sees me under that light, I don't want him to see me getting out of your car. I'll leave you right here, and then you go on home."

She refused to listen to this last. "All right," I said reluctantly. "But if there's any uproar, get out fast, because I won't come back to the car. You've done too much for me now, and I don't intend to get you in trouble."

I waited another two or three minutes while my nerves tied themselves in knots. The street remained silent and deserted. I'd better go now, before I got too scared to go at all. I eased the door open and slipped out. "Good luck," she whispered.

I came out from under the shadow of the trees at the intersection and felt a million eyes on me as I crossed Westbury under the street light. I hurried into the doorway. The door was locked. I pressed several buttons at random, and waited, feeling the muscles in my back grow taut. The door buzzed. I yanked it open, slipped inside, and hurried up the carpeted steps to the second floor.

The corridor was deserted. Apartment 2C was the second door on the left. I pressed the buzzer, and put one hand on the knob. For a moment nothing happened. It occurred to me that if they had safety chains on the doors I was sunk. Then I heard her moving. "Who's there?" she asked. I mumbled something indistinguishable and trusted to curiosity. The knob turned.

Her breath sucked in as I came in on her, but before the scream could cut loose I clamped a hand over her mouth. She fought, her eyes wide with terror as she recognized me. I shoved the door shut with my foot, and backed her across the room toward an armchair near the old-style pull-down bed. A small, rose-shaded lamp was burning on the table beside it. So far we hadn't made any noise, but I wasn't sure how long my luck would last; it was a very small room, too cluttered with furniture for much romping. I pushed her down in the chair with my hand still over her mouth, pinching her nostrils to shut off her breath.

"I'm not going to hurt you," I snapped. "Keep quiet, and I'll let you go." She quit fighting. I turned her loose, but stood over her ready to grab her again. My hand I'd had over her face was greasy with cold cream. She wore nothing but bra and pants and a sheer nylon robe or peignoir deal that had got wrapped around her waist in the struggle. She squirmed in the chair and tugged at it, trying to get some random bit of it down over her legs. The blonde hair was aswirl across her face, and the normally rather sullen brown eyes were crawling with fear as she looked up at me. "Wh-what are you going to do?"

"Nothing except ask you a few questions," I said. "But this time I want some answers, or I'll break you in two. You got me into this mess, and now you're going to get me out. Who was the man coming to Frances' apartment there in the shop when you were working for her?"

"I don't know," she said.

"You said there was one."

Her eyes avoided mine. "So maybe I was mistaken."

"But you weren't; and that's what intrigues me. Apparently you were the only one who ever found it out, but *how* did you? Did you ever see him?"

"No."

"Were you ever back there in the apartment?"

"Once or twice. With her."

"See any men's clothing lying around? Cigar butts? Pipes?"

She shook her head.

"I see," I said. "Now, at that time Frances and I were dating pretty steadily and generally considered to be engaged, so if you *had* seen any evidence a man had been in her apartment, you'd just have assumed it was me, wouldn't you?"

"Well, yes—I guess so."

"Good." Now we were getting somewhere. "But when you told me about it on the phone, you obviously didn't mean me. So you must have meant you had reason to believe there was a man in her apartment on some night when it *couldn't* have been me? When maybe I was out of town?"

She hesitated. "Look—maybe I was wrong—"

"No, you weren't. You were dead right, and I'll tell you how you knew. Junior Delevan was a pretty big boy, wasn't he?"

She gasped. "I don't know anything about that business!"

"Too big to be killed, and then loaded into a car, by a 120-pound girl, wouldn't you say?"

"I tell you, I don't know anything about—"

"Maybe you don't. But I'll bet you could make a pretty good guess as to where he went that night Couldn't you?"

Her gaze went past me, crawling sickly around the room, looking for some way out. "I—I didn't even see him at all that night. You can ask the police. You can ask his mother—"

I got it then, the thing I'd been trying to remember, the missing fragment that made a whole picture of it when you put it in place. I grinned coldly down at her. "That's right. You phoned his house twice, didn't you, trying to get hold of him?"

"That's right. We had a date. He was supposed to pick me up when the store closed, but he didn't come."

"Quite a night for being stood up, wasn't it, Doris?"

"What do you mean?"

"I broke a date with Frances, too, remember?"

"No. Why should I?" She tried to brazen it out, but her eyes shifted, avoiding mine.

"You remember, all right. You were in the shop Friday afternoon when I stopped there and asked her to go to a dance Saturday night at the Rutherford Country Club."

"So maybe I was. I worked there, didn't I?"

"Did you say anything about it to Junior?"

"How do I know?"

"*Did you?*"

"How you expect me to remember all the things we talked about? You think I write down every word I say to anybody?"

"You told him, all right."

"Have it your way; so all we got to talk about is you and your crummy dates, big-wheel Warren. How would I remember? And if I did, it's a Federal case, I suppose?"

"I don't know," I said. "Scanlon could answer that question for you. But let's get on to the big item. You were also in the shop around eight P.M. Saturday when I came by to tell Frances I had to go to Tampa and couldn't make the dance. And you've just said you didn't see Junior at all that night. You tried twice to call him at his home, so you must have had something very important to tell him, didn't you?"

She said nothing. Her hands began twisting at the robe; she'd forgotten about trying to cover up her legs, even if she remembered she had any.

"You never did get hold of Junior," I went on, "so it's obvious he never was warned she was going to be home that night, after all. And the next morning they found him on the city dump with his roof knocked in. Did you know he was going to burglarize the place that night, or just the first night she happened to be away?"

"Junior wouldn't—"

"The hell Junior wouldn't! He already had a previous conviction for burglary. And this time he even had a girlfriend who could get him a key. Or did he just break in?"

The truth was written on her face, but she tried to bluff it out. "I don't know what you're talking about!"

"Since she couldn't have done it, you knew there had to be a man there. *Do you know who he was?*"

"No! And you can't prove any of that junk—!"

I grabbed for her to shake the truth out of her, forgetting she didn't have on much to take hold of, and this time she cut loose with the scream. It must have come from her insteps, growing in volume all the way. I tried to get a hand over her mouth, stupidly hanging onto the bra and a handful of robe with the other, but the chair went over backward, taking the table and the lamp. The straps of the bra gave way and it all came off in my hand. She threw in another hopper of decibels and let go again, and bounced up and across the bed. I was as crazy now as she was, with no idea of what I was doing. I grabbed for her and got part of the robe just as she hit the floor on the other side of the bed and went rolling and bucking across the room, and then she was in the bathroom with the door locked, still screaming.

I wheeled and lunged for the door. There was nobody in the upper hall yet, but my luck ran out when I hit the bottom of the stairs. One man was already out of his apartment and another had his head out the door. They both recognized me, and yelled.

Probably at the moment all either wanted to do was get out of my way, since I was a madman who'd already killed two people and now possibly a third, but the one in the hallway dodged the same way I did and I was going too fast to swerve. I crashed into him and we went down.

Other doors were opening now, up and down the corridor, and a woman with a voice like an air-raid siren was shrieking, "*Call the police! Call the police!*" Just as I untangled myself and scrambled to my feet, the other man, braver now that reinforcements were in sight, came lunging at me. I knocked him down, but stepped backward and fell over the one who was under me. I bounced up, swung at the other who was already getting to his knees, knocked him over again, and plunged on toward the front door. Another man, in nothing but a pair of jockey shorts, was coming at a hard run now, from the far end of the hall.

I hit the front door at full speed, remembering too late that it opened inward, and slammed into it with my shoulder. Glass shattered and rained with a brittle tinkling sound on the tile. I yanked it open and leaped down the steps. Off to the left, as I ran across the street, I saw Barbara pulling out from the curb in the middle of the block. I made a desperate motion of the arm for her to get away, and ran up Westbury. I looked over my shoulder and saw her headlights swinging as she turned into it behind me. I plunged behind a hedge just before the lights caught up with me, and lay down on the ground. She went on past. I prayed she'd get out of the area before the police cars got here. She turned right at the next corner. People were still shouting and pouring out of the apartment house behind me, but none crossed the street. I cut across the yard I was in just as lights began to come on in the house, climbed the fence, and ran across the vacant lot behind it. When I emerged on the next street, there was no one in sight, but

I could already hear the sirens. A police car shot past on Taylor, off to my left I ran to the right and crossed Clebourne.

I heard a car coming this way. There were street lights ahead and behind me. I ducked into the alley back of Clebourne and fell flat behind some garbage cans, sobbing for breath. As the car went past its spotlight raked the shadows, but missed me. I lay still for a moment, trying to collect my wits after all we confusion. I couldn't go back to the office, even if I could get there. They'd search it, along with the house. But the Duquesne Building was in the next block; all I had to do was keep to the alley, cross one street, and I'd be behind it. I got up and ran again. The intersecting street was clear. I made it across, and ran on toward Montrose. I ducked into the small vestibule at the rear of the building, and collapsed, too winded to move. A car went past on Montrose, flashing its spotlight up the alley.

The door to the left opened onto the stairs going up to the second floor; the one on the right was the rear entrance to Roberts' apartment, leading into the kitchen. When I could get to my feet, I backed up as far as I could and crashed into the latter with my shoulder. On the third lunge the bolt tore out and it swung open. I stepped inside, closed it, and flicked on the cigarette lighter to look about for something to prop it shut. There was a small table next to the refrigerator. I shoved it against the door, holding the lighter with the other hand, and then stood looking down at the linoleum in horror. There were spatters of blood on it. The lighter went out. I flicked it on again. The blood was coming from a cut on the back of my left hand. I'd left a trail of it all the way from that apartment house that a Boy Scout could follow. I let the lighter go out and stood listening to the drip, drip, drip, as it fell and spattered in the darkness. Even if I could move on the streets now, there was nowhere else to go.

CHAPTER 10

WELL, I'D KNOWN ALL THE time they had to get me sooner or later. There was no use standing here crying about it; at least I could make use of the little time I had left. I looked at my watch; it was twenty minutes of four. The chances were they wouldn't discover that trail of blood until after daybreak, which was another three hours.

I groped my way to the bathroom. There was no window here, and I could turn on a light. I washed the blood off my hand. It was only a superficial cut from a piece of that falling glass; in all the uproar I'd been so charged with adrenalin I hadn't even felt it. I rooted around in his medicine chest for a Band-aid and stuck it on, but the blood continued to ooze out around the edges, so I wrapped a towel around it. I wouldn't bleed to death from a scratch like that.

There were two windows in the apartment, one in the living room-bedroom, facing Montrose, and the other in the kitchen, looking out into the alley. I closed the door from the kitchen, tore a blanket off the bed and draped it across the curtain rods of the window in here to cut off any seepage of light, and switched on a lamp. The furnishings were meager; it wouldn't take long to search the place. A dresser stood against the front wall, next to the door going out into the shop. The bed was in the corner beside it, under the window. At the foot of the bed was the door to the bathroom, with a small clothes closet beside it, while a desk stood against the wall opposite the window.

I started with the dresser drawers, and by the time I'd finished them I knew somebody had beaten me to it Whoever it was had made some effort to replace things with at least a semblance of order, but there was no doubt the place had been gone over. If there'd been any clue here as to Frances' identity or how Roberts had learned it, there was slight chance it was here now. He'd had two nights. Getting in had been no problem, apparently; if he'd had a key when Frances was living here, he probably still had it. The locks hadn't been changed. Then I remembered Scanlon and Ernie had been in here looking for the name and address of Roberts' next of kin. Maybe that was all it was. I moved on to the desk.

In the drawer were a dozen or more letters, thrown in haphazardly in their envelopes after he'd read them. Two were from his brother in Houston and were apparently the ones from which Scanlon had obtained the address. The others were all from girls, mostly in Houston and Galveston, handwritten on a variety of different pastel shades of stationery—though several of them would have been safer written on asbestos—and through all of them ran the same complaint: why didn't he write? Apparently he'd had a way with women, all right, but when they were out of sight he forgot about them. I skimmed through them hastily, reading a line or two in each paragraph and tossing them back into the drawer, not really expecting to find anything that had any bearing on his murder. The last one I picked up was postmarked Los Angeles sometime in November and in addition to being written on rough lavender paper it was perfumed. It was only three pages. I raced through it and had already tossed it aside in disgust when I did a double take over a word on the last page. "... *clippings...*"

Clippings?

I grabbed the letter up again.

"...you rascal, you never have even acknowledged those clippings you asked me for last summer, and when I think of the trouble—and risk—I went through to get them for you, well, honestly, I think you're a cad, sir. That's spelled s-t-i-n-k-e-r. The librarian almost caught me cutting them out of the papers in the file, and wouldn't my face have been red? At least you could tell me whether they were the ones you wanted—and also, Mr. Mysterious Roberts, what you wanted them for. Don't tell me you know the girl! Because if you do, I don't know whether to be worried about you, or just jealous. She must have been really something, in spades, and a dreamboat for looks, judging from the pictures. That is, if you like the type. Meow! Now you write to me, you villain, and tell me all..."

I threw the letter aside and began pawing through the drawer again. There were no clippings, and no other letter postmarked Los Angeles. I yanked the drawer out and looked under it to see if they were stuck to the bottom. I swung back to the dresser and did the same with the drawers in it. There was nothing. I went through them again, more thoroughly this time, unfolding the clean shirts, unrolling socks, and tearing out the paper liners in the bottom. I tore the bed apart and examined the mattress, searched the pockets of the suits hanging in the closet and felt the linings of the jackets. The knowledge that what I sought had actually been here was maddening. Well, they might still be here; there was still a chance he hadn't found them either. I went through the two suitcases in the closet and poked at the linings, tore the papers off the shelves, looked in the sweatbands of the two hats I found, lifted the dresser and the desk away from the wall and searched behind them, tore up the rug, turned over the chairs and checked their cushions, examined the wallpaper, looked in the water tank of the toilet in the bathroom, and under the old-fashioned tub. I peered through the barrels of two shotguns, and felt inside rubber boots. I couldn't turn on a light in the kitchen without blanking off the window, but I'd found a flashlight that would be safe enough, so I started out there, tearing papers out of cupboards, looking in cereal boxes and in the stove and refrigerator, even in the icecube trays, and minutely examining the linoleum for traces of its having been disturbed. I found nothing. If he'd kept the clippings here, George had already got them.

I went back into the other room, closed the kitchen door, and slumped wearily on the bed. It was four-thirty; it had taken almost an hour. A car went past on Montrose, its tires squealing as it made the turn into Clebourne. In my mind I could see them criss-crossing the town, flashing their lights into doorways and shrubbery, blocking the exits. *Take no chances; he's insane, and he may be armed.*

I craned my neck and stared up at the ceiling. George's offices were directly over my head. Reaching over on the desk for the phone, I looked up the number in the directory dialed it, and sat smiling bitterly as I listened to it ring. I shrugged, and let the receiver drop back on the cradle.

I'd better call Barbara and remind her. She should be back at her apartment by now. She answered on the first ring. "Hello?"

"Duke—"

"Oh, thank Heaven! I've been scared blue. Where are you?"

"In Roberts' apartment. Look—they're going to find my suitcase in the office. Remember, stick to your story and there's nothing they can do; there was no way you could have known I was back there—"

She cut me off. "Never mind that. What did you find out from Doris?"

I told her. "She won't admit it, but she knows Junior broke in here that night to burglarize the place. She wasn't able to get hold of him to tell him I'd had to break the date with Frances, so he thought he was going to have the place to himself and could find where she kept the Saturday receipts from the shop. But of course he walked in on two people, and I don't think there's any doubt now the other one was George. I just checked, and you can hear the phone in his office from down here. For having a girlfriend on the side, in a small town, you'd never find a cozier arrangement. I suppose he worked a lot at night."

"Yes, and usually alone. I used to see the windows lighted at night when I'd be coming home from a date or from a movie. He never asked for any stenographic help, so I just assumed he was reading law on cases he was working on."

"It was a beautiful set-up, all right. If anybody—Fleurelle, for instance—tried to call him, all he had to do was go out through the kitchen, up the stairs, and answer it. But when Junior walked in on them that night, he must have lost his head. I doubt he intended to kill him—he was just taken by surprise and hit him too hard with something. They probably didn't have any trouble getting the body out of here, since they could bring the car into the alley right to the back door, but from then on there was a lot more at stake than a scandal and divorce."

"Then on top of that, she pulled out of the arrangement and married you."

"Right. So all George had for his trouble was a potential murder charge hanging over his head—"

She broke in, "And Roberts probably didn't even know about that part of it at all."

I grinned coldly. It was hard to imagine sympathizing with a blackmailer, but you could almost feel sorry for poor Roberts. He had a nice safe racket going, extorting money from a girl standing in front of him, and all the time he was inadvertently threatening to expose a homicide committed by a very dangerous man standing behind him. "It's a miracle he lasted as long as he did. That's actually what got him killed—the fact he didn't know George had any connection with her at all. But if he exposed her, the whole thing might come out. What he was gouging her for, God only knows, except that it must have been something that happened before she ever came here."

"But how do you suppose Roberts could have found out about that?"

I told her about the letter from the girl in Los Angeles and its reference to clippings. "I've searched every inch of the apartment and there are no clippings here, so Roberts either kept them somewhere else or George beat me to 'em. It still doesn't make much sense, anyway; the news stories could only verify something Roberts already suspected, but she came here from Florida, he was from Texas, and the clippings must have been from a California paper. Naturally, I was hoping that one of those detectives in Miami or Houston would turn up some lead that would indicate she and Roberts had known each other before, but since that didn't pan out we're still as far from home as ever."

"Except for one thing. Roberts was a policeman at one time."

"Yes, there's still that."

"What happened in Doris' apartment?"

"I pulled one of my dumb stunts," I said ruefully. I told her about reaching for her to shake her. "So when about the last stitch she had on came off in my hand—"

"Yes, hardly anything would be more calculated to reassure a girl already about to jump out of her skin than tearing off her bra. But never mind; what do we do now?"

"Now?" I said. "You're going to keep denying you even knew I was in town. And I'm going to thank you for all you've done. Over and out."

"But can't we tell Scanlon what we've found out?"

"We can't prove a word of it. And besides, there's nothing so far even to indicate George killed Frances, or any reason he would have—"

"Reason? He hated her."

"Maybe, but there's no proof. George is a lawyer, and he's covered in every direction. He's too smart to leave anything to chance."

"But he's already made one mistake we know of. When he killed Roberts, that thing about the different-sized shot."

"It was a minor one, and nothing that'd ever tie it to him. Anyway, they'll be here before long."

"They'll never think to look for you there."

I told her about cutting my hand. "As soon as it's light they'll pick up the trail and follow me right in here."

"But maybe I could pick you up there at the mouth of the alley—"

I interrupted her. "Not a chance. They've got the whole town staked out by now, and anything moving will be stopped and searched; they've probably got road-blocks on the highway. There's nowhere to go, anyway. Thanks again for everything,

Barbara. You've been wonderful." I hung up before she could protest.

I sagged wearily down on the bed, past all caring, and stared at the blood-soaked towel around my hand. Footsteps scuffed along the alley, and I heard another car go careening up Montrose. Somewhere a man shouted. I looked around at the mess I'd made of the room searching it, and groped in my pockets for a cigarette. The pack was empty. I wadded it up and threw it in a corner. Well, at least they'd come out even—the cigarettes, and the short happy life of John Duquesne Warren. The telephone rang. I reached over listlessly and picked it up.

"Listen, Duke," she said excitedly, "I'm going to tell them where you are."

"I hadn't thought of that," I said. "It's a good idea; it should get you off the hook—"

"Please! Will you stop talking about that? If they're going to find you before long anyway, we have nothing to lose. I've got the glimmerings of an idea, and I need some leverage."

"What is it?"

"No, don't get your hopes up; it has about one chance in a thousand. But you don't have any where you are now. Is it a deal?"

"Sure."

"Good. Now, listen—tell Scanlon what you've found out about Junior, and about anything else you want, but don't express any suspicion of George at all. There's another man mixed up in it, but you have no idea who he is. You want George to defend you, and you want him there when they question you. Insist on it."

"Okay," I said. I couldn't even guess what she had in mind, but as she pointed out I had nothing to lose.

"Good luck," she said softly. The receiver clicked.

Five minutes passed. I sat waiting for the sound of sirens. They'd converge on the building, surround it, throw their spotlights on the doors, and order me to come out with my hands in the air. The phone rang again.

I picked it up. "Hello."

"Mr. Warren, listen—this is Barbara Ryan. I want to talk to you; it's very important. I'm calling from the sheriff's office, but don't cut me off till I explain." I frowned. What was the matter with her? I opened my mouth to say something, but she went right on talking, not giving me a chance.

"...I had to do it, Mr. Warren. I had to; it was the only way. I told them where you are. And I want you to promise me you won't do anything rash. I'm trying to help you, if you'll listen to me."

It began to soak in then. Scanlon would be on another extension, and she was talking fast to keep me from saying anything until she could get her message over.

"...you've got to give yourself up. This thing can be solved, if you just go at it the right way, with people helping you. We'll get detectives, and lawyers. You won't be alone. But if you try to resist, you'll be killed; you won't have a chance. Mr. Scanlon is going to move his men into the area in another few minutes, but I told him if I could talk to you first maybe I could get you to come out. Just don't resist. Promise me that."

I wondered what I was going to resist with, even if I were stupid enough to consider it, and then it occurred to me I was in the back room of a sporting goods store and just on the other side of the door were several thousand dollars' worth of guns and ammunition. I was finally beginning to catch up. Scanlon was convinced I was insane, and could understandably be nervous about sending men into a dark building after a maniac with an arsenal at his disposal. Leverage, she'd said. She wanted something from him, and this was the way she was prying it out of him.

Well, at least I could help her a little. Also, the thought that Scanlon was listening made it irresistible. "What chance have I got after they get hold of me?" I snarled. "That bunch of meat-headed clowns in the Sheriff's Department couldn't find their way out of a phone booth. Why bother to try to solve the thing when they've got me? They might have to get off their big, fat, political—"

Scanlon's voice broke in. "You'd better listen to her, Warren. If we have to come in there after you, or drive you out with tear gas—"

"Please, Mr. Scanlon, let me do the talking!" I heard her plead in the background, as though she'd covered the mouthpiece of her extension. He shut up, and her voice came up clear again, begging me to give myself up.

"Well, wait a minute," I said. "Not so fast. For one thing, I want a lawyer. I'm a little fed up with being accused of all the crimes committed in this county."

"You'll have a lawyer. I'll call anybody you want."

"I want George Clement," I said. "And I want him there from the start. They're not going to railroad me."

'I'll call Mr. Clement right now. Will you do it, Mr. Warren?"

I hesitated a moment. "Well, all right," I said grudgingly. "Tell 'em I'll come out the front door with my hands up."

"Thank God!"

There was so much fervent and heart-felt relief in it she almost convinced me. I let the receiver drop back in the cradle, feeling like Dillinger or Machine-Gun Kelly, and wondering what the odds were on anyone's refusing that girl anything she decided she wanted. Before they came, I unwound the towel from my hand. With that build-up, they might think I had a gun concealed in it.

I sat back down on the bed again, aware that for the first time in a self-sufficient life I was completely dependent on somebody else. I didn't have the slightest idea as to what she was up to; the only thing apparent was that she had to have either Scanlon's permission or help, or both. I started back over everything we'd found out, searching for the glimmer of light she'd spotted and that I'd missed, but gave it up. It only made my head ache. Strangely, I didn't doubt her at all. That was the only thing I was sure of; she *had* seen something. She hadn't turned me in merely to get out from under a charge of harboring a fugitive.

They were there in less than five minutes. They converged on the building, surrounded it, threw their spotlights on the doors, and ordered me to come out with my hands in the air.

CHAPTER 11

"QUIET!" SCANLON ROARED. "Mulholland, get those damned people out of here and close the doors. And tell Simpson to keep the corridor clear out there. Nobody can even get in or out of this madhouse."

It was growing light now beyond the dusty windows of the courthouse; Sunday morning had dawned at last. The cut on my hand had been stitched and bandaged. I was handcuffed, sitting at one of the desks in the sheriff's office. Scanlon and Howard Brill, another of his deputies, were keeping an eye on me from opposite sides of the desk, while Mulholland and another man struggled with the crowd surging in through the doors and threatening to overrun the railing and counter inside the entrance. Scanlon's face was lined with fatigue, the eyes red from lack of sleep. I had an idea I looked just as bad, or worse.

I lit a cigarette from the pack someone had given me. It was awkward in the handcuffs. Brill pushed an ashtray toward me, his face reflecting the mingled revulsion and pity with which laymen regard the dangerously insane; he hadn't been a policeman long enough to have acquired the necessary objectivity. I paid no attention. I was too busy with my own bleak thoughts and trying to guess what Barbara was up to. She was nowhere in sight, and hadn't been here when they brought me in. I supposed she'd gone home.

Mulholland had got the doors closed now and come back. He looked at me, shook his head, and sat down on the corner of another desk. The scuffling of feet and the sound of protesting voices and shouted questions had begun to subside out in the corridor as Simpson pushed back the crowd. Scanlon said something.

"What?" I asked.

"Do you want to make a statement?" he repeated.

"Yes," I said. "I want to make three. I didn't kill my wife. I didn't kill Roberts. And I want George Clement."

Mulholland sighed. "Here we go again."

Scanlon took a cigar from his pocket and bit the end off it, regarding me with the blank impersonality of a camera lens. We'd been friends a long time, but he was a professional from the boot-heels up, and if you took the money you did the job. You could get sick later, in private. He struck a match and held it in front of the cigar. "Clement's on his way over here now."

Well, he shouldn't be long, I thought; this time he didn't have to stop and kill anybody on the way. Just then, there was a commotion at the door as he came in, readjusting the set of his jacket after pushing through the crowd outside. His face was composed and sympathetic as he came over to me. I stood up and we shook hands, a little awkwardly in the handcuffs. She'd said to play it this way. The least I could do was try.

"I'm sorry about this, Duke," he said in the comforting tone a veterinarian would use to an animal with a broken leg. "The whole thing's obviously a mistake that'll be cleared up. I can't interfere with the investigation, of course, but I'll be here in case you need me."

"Fine," I said. "I knew I could count on you. And I'm sure it's just as obvious to you as it is to me that the way to clear it up is to find out who killed Roberts and Frances, and why. I think I know why, and if we could get a little help from the police—"

Scanlon cut me off coldly. "That'll do, Warren. You're not here to make a speech. You're under arrest for suspicion of murder, and I have to warn you that anything you say can be used against you. Do you want to make a statement?"

"I've already made it. I had nothing to do with those murders. And if you'll get Doris Bentley in here—"

"Never mind Doris Bentley."

"Do you want to solve this thing, or don't you?"

"You've got enough charges against you now, without attempted rape. So far, she hasn't filed a complaint, but I wouldn't crowd my luck if I were you."

"Did she tell you what I went there to see her about?"

"She said you tried to rape her."

"That's all?"

"Maybe she thought that covered it. You broke into her room at three o'clock in the morning and started tearing her clothes off; if you were just trying to get her recipe for meat loaf, you should have said so."

George had sat down at another desk off to my left. I stole a glance at him as I said to Scanlon, "I still think you'd better get her in here. She might be able to tell you where Junior Delevan was killed that night."

Scanlon's eyes narrowed. "What's that?"

There wasn't a quiver in George's face. He merely glanced curiously in my direction as though wondering why I'd dragged that in.

"And Doris," I went on, "is also the girl who called you Thursday night and told you I killed Roberts because he was having an affair with my wife." If I couldn't get action one way, I could in another.

"How did you know about that?" Scanlon barked.

"Because she also called me."

"Before your wife came home?"

"That's right."

That did it. Without turning his head, Scanlon snapped to Mulholland. "Get that girl in here."

Mulholland went out, on the double. When Scanlon used that tone, he meant jump, and jump fast.

I turned to George. "I realize I'm probably making your job tougher, but it was necessary." Obviously, Doris' confirmation of the telephone call to me would nail down the two things the prosecution would be overjoyed to prove: motive and premeditation. "But since I didn't kill her," I went on, "it doesn't make any difference anyway."

They all looked at me pityingly—everybody except George. He took a cigarette from a silver case, studied it thoughtfully as he tapped it on a thumbnail, and said, "Well, my hands are more or less tied here, Duke, since I can't interfere with the investigation, but perhaps it would have been better…" He let his voice trail off. In other words: *I'll do my best, but you've probably already hanged yourself.*

We waited. I wondered if I could break her down when she got here; if she managed to brazen it out, it'd just be my word against hers. Maybe I could get some help from Scanlon; he was too brainy an investigator to ignore a lead in an unsolved murder case, even if it came from an obvious madman. In less than ten minutes they pushed through the crowd in the corridor and came in; Mulholland apparently hadn't given her time to do more than throw some clothes on. She had on no makeup, and her hair was sloppily combed, which probably wasn't going to help her morale any. I could tell she was scared, all right; she was trying to look tough and assured, but was merely defiant as they came over to the desk. She glanced at me and then quickly away before I could meet her eye.

"I didn't want to file any charges," she said sullenly. "He's just a nut."

"That's not what we wanted to see you about," Scanlon told her. "Are you the girl who called here the other night and told us Mrs. Warren had been visiting Dan Roberts' apartment?"

For a moment I thought she was going to deny it. Then she looked bitterly at me, and said, "I suppose he accused me of it?"

"Never mind. Did you?"

"All right, what if I did? It's true."

"I see. And you also called Warren, and said the same thing?"

"Yes." She was in now, so there was no use denying that part.

"Was it before you called us, or after?"

"It was before."

"Do you remember the time exactly?"

"Not exactly, but it was between ten and eleven. About twenty minutes before I called you."

Scanlon nodded. "And you'd be prepared to testify to that under oath?"

"Will I have to?"

"Probably. If it's the truth, there's no reason you shouldn't, is there?"

"No-o, I guess not. It's the truth, all right."

Scanlon was silent for a moment, just watching her. Then he asked, "When you called Warren, did you identify yourself?"

"No," she said.

"I see. Then how did he know it was you?"

"I guess he recognized my voice."

"But when he broke into your room this morning, he didn't say anything about that? He just tried to rape you?"

She hesitated. She wasn't a very imaginative liar. "Well, he started tearing my clothes off—"

"Don't you think it's more likely he intended to kill you? Your testimony might convict him of murder."

She brightened. "Yes, maybe that was it. I bet that's why he grabbed me."

"Probably. How long would you say he'd been in the room when he made this grab for you?"

"Maybe five minutes. Not much longer."

"That's a little odd, isn't it? Why do you suppose he wasted so much time?"

You could see her realizing she'd made a mistake, after it was too late. "Well, I don't know. Maybe it wasn't that long."

"Ummm. It was more like—three minutes, maybe?"

"Yeah. That was probably it. About three minutes."

"I see. But that still seems like quite a while for a man to horse around with small talk when he's going to kill a girl in an apartment house with people asleep just on the other side of the wall. You'd think he'd want to get the show on the road before you could scream. And, incidentally, why didn't you? No—wait—at that time you didn't know he intended to kill you. You just thought he was going to rape you."

"Uh—yes. That was it."

"Why? At that time, he still hadn't grabbed you."

"Well—I really didn't know *what* he wanted."

"But you must have wondered? I mean, there didn't seem to be much chance he was looking for the bus station, or just wanted to borrow something to read. What did you talk about during this period? He must have said something."

"Well, just some of his nutty stuff, I guess; he's crazier'n a bedbug. And I was too scared to remember—"

"But what kind of nutty stuff? You must remember a word or two. Did he mention Junior Delevan?"

Her eyes avoided his as they began that characteristic circuit of the wall behind him, seeking some way out. She said nothing. I shot an oblique glance at George. He'd realized long since where this was heading, but his face expressed nothing but an intelligent professional interest.

"Well, did he?" Scanlon prodded.

"Well—"

"Did he?"

"I guess—maybe he did—"

"Why?"

"Well, how would I know?" she asked sullenly.

Scanlon's cigar had gone out. He removed it from his mouth and regarded the wet end of it thoughtfully. "You run into some weird ones in this business, Doris, but this one may take the Scanlon Award for 1961. How are you going to account for a man breaking into the room of a pretty girl like you at three o'clock in the morning and tearing her clothes off just to talk about Junior Delevan?" Suddenly, without any warning at all, his flattened hand came down on top of the desk with a sound like a pistol shot and his voice lashed out. *"What did he ask you about Delevan?"*

That was all it took. She came apart like a cheap toy that'd been left out in the rain. In less than five minutes he had the whole conversation.

"Did Junior ever ask you what that shop took in on an average Saturday?" he demanded.

She was crying now. "Well, he might have. It was a long time ago."

"Did he have a key to the place?"

"No," she said. "I m-mean, I don't know."

"Did you have one?"

"No. Of course not. She lived there, so she always opened up."

"Then how did Delevan get one?"

"He d-didn't."

"I think he did. There has to be some reason you never did tell us you suspected he was killed in the back of that shop, something that involves guilty knowledge on your part. Either you planned the burglary with him, or you had reason to believe he was going to do it himself. Maybe it was only the fact you didn't want to have to admit you knew he had a key. Where'd he get it? Did you steal it for him?"

"No! I didn't do any such thing."

"Did he ever have a chance to get his hands on her keys?"

She hesitated fearfully. "Wh-what will they do to me?"

"I can't make any promises, but probably nothing, if you tell us."

"All right. But I didn't have anything to do with it."

"Just tell us."

"It was one day when she was out somewhere and she'd left her keys on the showcase next to the cash register. Junior was there, talking to me, and then a customer came in. While I was waiting on her, I happened to look over where he was, and he'd taken out his chewing gum and was pressing one of the keys into it."

"And when was this?" Scanlon asked.

"About two weeks before—before he was killed."

"And you never did tell her—Frances Kinnan, I mean?"

She began to cry again. "I was afraid to. Junior could be real mean when he wanted to."

Scanlon gestured wearily. "All right, you can go."

She went out. He relit his cigar, and sighed. "We'll never be able to prove a word of it."

"That's right," I said. "Unless you catch the man that was in the apartment with Frances that night, the man who killed him. And for once you can look somewhere else. I was in Tampa, Florida."

He gestured impatiently. "Hell, it hasn't got anything to do with this, anyway."

I banged my manacled hands on the desk. "Dammit, it has everything to do with it!"

"Oh, cut it out," he snapped. "You killed Roberts because you thought he was having an affair with your wife. And you killed her for the same reason. All this guesswork about Delevan and where he was or wasn't killed that night doesn't change the facts in the slightest. You haven't got a chance in the world, so why don't you come clean and get it over with?"

It had all been for nothing, I thought. I wondered where Barbara was and what she was trying to do. Well, it really didn't matter; nothing would help me. "Listen to me a minute," I said wearily, knowing before I started it was futile. "I'll try to explain it in words of one syllable. Roberts was blackmailing her. Not because of Delevan, because he didn't know anything about that. But because of something else that happened before she ever came here; the thing, whatever it was, that made her change her name. If we ever find out who she really was, and who brought her here—"

"We know who she was," he said.

I stared at him. "You do? How?"

"The F.B.I. identified her from that photograph you gave Norman. They've got quite a file on her."

"Embezzlement?" I asked.

He shook his head. "No. I thought that myself, when I heard about the ponies, but it's not that simple. As a matter of fact, in 25 years in this business, I don't think I've ever seen a package quite like it. Her name's Elena Mallory—or that was the one she started with; she's added to it from time to time."

I shot a glance at George. Other than well-bred curiosity, his face showed nothing at all. Maybe we were wrong, after all.

Scanlon went on. "She seems to be wanted, under various names and at various times since 1954, by the State of Nevada, the State of California, the Internal Revenue Service, the F.B.I., and the U.S. Immigration and Naturalization Service, for fraud, evasion of income tax, hit-and-run driving, manslaughter, illegal flight to escape prosecution, bigamy, and deportation as an undesirable alien. I suppose if she were still alive they'd have to cut cards for her."

My gears became meshed at last. "Bigamy?"

"Yes. She seems to have been a girl who was easily bored. As I get the picture, she was a Guatemalan citizen, of Irish and Spanish parentage, educated in the United States—that is, until she ran away from the last school they put her in and married some horse-trainer on the California racing circuit. He lost his license for giving stimulants to a horse—which he says she did—and later, without bothering to divorce him, she married, a Southern California used-car dealer who was pretty well-to-do, or was until she got her scoop into his bankroll and started heaving it into the pari-mutuel windows at Santa Anita and Hollywood Park. Then she wrote several thousand dollars worth of rubber checks at casinos at Las Vegas, and ran over and killed a man with her sports car, and took it on the lam. This last item was in October, 1958. They've been looking for her ever since, waiting for her to drop the other shoe; sooner or later she figured to be back in the headlines. She was reported to have been seen at a Florida horse track in December, 1958, but disappeared before they could get their hands on her. That would have been just a few weeks before she showed up here."

That tied it all together, I thought—and we'd never prove a bit of it. He really must have hated her. He'd picked her up broke in Florida and set her up in the dress shop. Then in less than six months she'd ditched him and married me, sold the stock and fixtures, and kept the money herself, so all he'd got out of it was to put himself at the mercy of a reckless and irresponsible girl who might some day get him sent to prison for the death of Junior Delevan. With her record of unbuttoned and uninhibited behavior, there was no telling what she'd spill if the police ever caught up with her. And on top of that there was no doubt he'd had to keep paying Roberts off—through her—because she'd probably told him she'd already given Roberts everything she had. And then he learned from Denman she'd just dropped six or seven thousand dollars at the racetrack in New Orleans.

I looked at him now; he seemed perfectly at ease. Nothing would ever crack him. Well, Roberts was dead, and she was dead; he really didn't have much to be afraid of. Except maybe turning put the light at night.

At least I had to try. "All right," I said to Scanlon, "that accounts for Paul Denman. This man, whoever he was, knew the police would always be on the lookout for her around racetracks, so he hired Denman to follow her. And of course he found out it was exactly as he'd suspected; she was on another gambling binge, and sooner or later she'd be recognized and picked up. When she came home, he killed her. He even destroyed her photograph—the big one in the bedroom—to keep the newspapers from running it. Somebody might have recognized her. He didn't know I had a small one in my wallet."

Scanlon shook his head. "He couldn't have killed her. Nobody knew she was home. Except you."

The door opened then, and the Deputy on guard called but to Scanlon. "Mrs. Ryan's out here. She says she's got to see you or Mr. Clement."

"What about?" Scanlon asked.

"She says some evidence."

"All right. Let her in."

CHAPTER 12

I WAS CONSCIOUS OF THE shallowness of my breathing as I watched her come through the door. She looked lovely, but very tired. She smiled at me, and then nervously at the others as she came over to the desk. "Excuse me for interrupting, Mr. Scanlon, but I think I may have something important."

"What is it?" he asked.

She turned slightly to include George. "I don't know whether it would be classified as defense evidence or just evidence, but I thought the best thing would be to come here right away."

George smiled. "Any evidence is properly turned over to the police, Mrs. Ryan. If it's pertinent, we have access to it too."

Scanlon interrupted impatiently. "Sure, sure. But what is it?"

"Well, I've just been talking to Mr. Denman—you remember, the private detective. I called him last night to ask if he thought he'd recognize this Randall's voice if he heard it again, but he didn't think so—that is, he wouldn't be able to pick it out of a number of similar voices, and his testimony would probably have no value as evidence. So then I asked him about the envelope Randall sent the money in, but he said there was nothing there either. It was just a plain white envelope from the drugstore or dime store, and the address was typewritten. There was no return address, of

145

course, and no letter with it. Just the money. Then, a little while ago, it occurred to me that typewriters can be identified too. They all have their individual characteristics—"

"Yes, of course," Scanlon broke in. "The F.B.I, can do it, or any good police lab. But there's not a chance in the world he'd have it now. Nobody ever keeps an envelope."

"But that's just it," she said eagerly. "I think he does have it."

"What do you mean?"

"I just talked to him. At his home. He says he threw the envelope in the waste basket, all right, but the thing is he doesn't have any janitor service in the building where his office is, and he doesn't think he's emptied the basket since then—since Tuesday afternoon, when he got it. He's going down to the office in the next half hour or so, as soon as he's had breakfast, and he'll look and see if it's still there. I asked him to call you, if it is, and you'd tell him whether to turn it over to the F.B.I, or mail it to you in another envelope."

"Good. I'll call the F.B.I. myself, if he finds it." Scanlon removed the cold cigar from his mouth and regarded it musingly. He shook his head. "Faith is a wonderful thing, Mrs. Ryan. For your sake, I almost hope this doesn't backfire on you."

"I don't think it will," she said. She went out.

For a moment no one spoke. Then Scanlon relighted his cigar and smiled grimly at George. "I think this is one you're going to lose, counselor. If they identify that as one of the typewriters in Warren's office, on top of everything else we've got—there goes your ball game."

George shrugged easily. "Well, they haven't yet, remember. Don't try to bluff us with an empty gun."

I glanced at my watch. It was seven-thirty-five. *The next half hour or so*—I wondered if I'd live through it, or if I did, whether I'd ever be the same again. My nerve ends felt as if they were going to snap and come out through my skin like steel wire. George didn't even bother to look at his watch. He merely lit another cigarette and listened attentively as Scanlon took up the questioning again. A telephone stood on the desk between us like a silent black bomb, and there was another on the desk where he was sitting, next to his left elbow. He didn't look at either of them. Nor was there the slightest indication in his face that he was avoiding them.

We must be wrong, I thought; nobody has that kind of nerve. Or if we weren't, he must have weighed the possibilities and decided it was a bluff. No, I told myself; there was still a chance he was only timing it to get out gracefully, without suspicion. But, good God, how long could he wait? How long could he endure it?

Scanlon was saying something.

"What?"

His eyes were bleak as he leaned over the other end of the desk. "I hope we're not causing you any inconvenience, Warren, with all these silly questions. But there have been a couple of people killed, and the taxpayers always get into a snit about it and start saying we ought to look into it."

"All right," I said. "What do you want to know now?"

"I want to know if you're ready to make a statement."

"I don't know your definition of the word," I said, "but to the best of my knowledge I've been making statements ever since I was dragged in here. Apparently they go in one corner of your head, reverberate, and flow out the other, without causing a ripple—"

Seven-thirty-nine.

"How long are you going to hold out?"

"As long as I'm breathing. I've told you what happened."

"You're the only one in town who knew your wife was home. How could somebody else have killed her?"

"She called him. The minute I left the house with Mulholland."

"So she could get her head broken with an andiron? Now, that makes sense."

I explained about the fight. "Maybe she even thought I'd killed Roberts, from the way I was acting and from the fact I had the cigarette lighter, the one Doris told you about. It was a new one she'd ordered, but she didn't know that. Anyway, she had to get away—get away from me, and out of reach before you could question her about Roberts. But she didn't have any money left, and couldn't very well ask me for any, the way I was raving and breaking down doors, so she called this man, whoever he was."

"But why would he kill her, if she was leaving town anyway? She couldn't spill anything."

"Because he didn't trust her, for one thing; she was too reckless and unreliable. You read her record. She'd be picked up somewhere. Also, he hated her. You saw what he did to her face."

Seven-forty-four.

My hands, manacled together, lay on the edge of the desk. I could see the watch without moving my face. It had been nine minutes now...ten ...

The telephone rang, the sudden sound of it like an explosion in the room. If he doesn't scream now, and start across the ceiling, I thought, he has no nerves in his body at all. Or he's innocent. I glanced toward him. His face was utterly calm, as though he hadn't even heard it. No, he had turned slightly and was watching Scanlon as he picked up the receiver.

"Sheriff's office. Scanlon speaking—"

It didn't mean anything. Everybody was watching Scanlon.

"Yes, yes, I know," he said.

Out of the corner of my eye, I saw George take out a cigarette. Then he realized he already had one burning in the tray, and put it back.

"... but, dammit, honey, I can't get away. I realize I haven't had any breakfast. Or any sleep. I sometimes notice things like that, without help. But I'm not going to leave here till we crack this thing."

If it were me, I thought, they'd have heard the sigh of relief in Memphis. Nothing showed. Absolutely nothing.

Scanlon hung up. Then he sighed, and said, "All right, let's get on with it."

George glanced at his watch. "Speaking of breakfast—how long do you think it'll be, Sheriff, before I'll be able to talk to Duke?"

"Not for hours, at this rate," Scanlon said disgustedly.

George stood up. "Well, I think I'll run over to Fuller's and have a bite." He turned to me. "There's nothing I can do at the moment, Duke, and I'll be back in twenty minutes or so. You don't mind?"

"No," I said. I managed a sickly grin. "I'll try to hold off the wolves till you get back."

"Could I have Fuller's send you over something?"

"No, thanks. I couldn't eat anything."

He went out. There was a long moment's silence after the door closed behind him. Scanlon and Mulholland exchanged a glance. Scanlon jerked his head. Mulholland went out, and almost at the same instant Barbara came back in. She must have been in another room across the corridor. She came on around the desk and sat down on my right.

Scanlon spoke to Brill. "Get that line open to the radio room."

Brill stepped inside Scanlon's private office, leaving the door open. The three of us remained where we were, staring at the telephone on the desk between us.

Scanlon looked at Barbara, the gray eyes flinty. "I never thought I'd use the sheriff's office for a routine like this. If I didn't have a dirty hunch you could be right, I'd lock you up."

She made no reply. She glanced at me and tried to smile, but it didn't quite come off. A minute went by. At this hour on Sunday morning you could drive anywhere in town in less than three minutes. It had to be before then. Two minutes. The silence began to roar in my ears. The room was swollen and bulging with it, like some dark and suffocating pressure. Three minutes. I stared at the telephone, and then away, and back at it again. Barbara had lowered her head, and I saw her eyes were closed. Her elbows rested on the desk, and she was raising and lowering her fists, so tightly clenched the knuckles were white, bumping the heels of them gently against the wood in some rhythmic and supplicant cadence she apparently wasn't aware of or didn't know how to stop.

The telephone rang. I saw her gulp. Her shoulders shook, and she groped for her handkerchief and pressed it against her mouth.

Scanlon picked it up. He listened for a moment, said, "Thank you, operator," and called out to Brill, "Phone booth at Millard's Texaco Station, corner of Clebourne and Mason." She slid slowly down onto the desk with her head on her arms.

I heard Brill repeat the location into the other line for the radio dispatcher. Scanlon went on listening. Brill came back, picked up the phone on the adjoining desk, and listened also. In a moment Scanlon gestured toward the instrument, and pointed to me. Brill moved it over and gave me the receiver, motioning for me to keep quiet.

A man was speaking. "...don't really believe it's there, do you?" It was George's voice.

"Well, I'm not sure," another man's voice replied. "As I say, I was just leaving now to go down to the office and look."

"I'm almost certain it wouldn't be there after all this time. Are you by any chance a betting man, Mr. Denman?"

"Well, I've been known to take a little flyer now and then, when the odds are right. Why?"

"I'd be willing to make a pretty substantial wager that when you get down there you won't find it."

"Hmmm. And what's your definition of substantial, on an average Sunday?"

"Say two thousand dollars?"

"Now, wait a minute, Mr. Randall. I understand that's a pretty heavy situation up there, and destroying evidence—"

"Who said anything about destroying evidence? You're just going down there to look for something the chances are you threw away five days ago. Suppose we make it four thousand you don't find it?"

"Five."

"All right. But understand, I'll never pay any more—"

There was something sounding like a scuffle then, and another voice came on the line. "I've got him." It was Mulholland.

"Good. Bring him in," Scanlon said. Then he added, "Thanks, Denman."

Denman chuckled. "Oh, you can tell Mrs. Ryan she'll get a bill. And Academy Award performances like that come high."

Scanlon hung up. Brill took the receiver out of my hand, put it down, and unlocked the handcuffs. I couldn't say anything. I reached over and put a hand on Barbara's shoulder.

She pushed herself erect, and looked at me. Her chin quivered, and tears were running down her face. "You nuh—nuh—nun—you nuh—need a shave," she said. "You look awful." Then she was up, and gone out the door.

She came back in a minute or two, apparently from the washroom down the corridor, with the tearstains erased and her lipstick on straight. She smiled and shook her head. "Sorry I went hysterical on you. But I guess I'm not built for that kind of pressure."

"Well, I'd had about all I could take, myself," I said.

"But it's all over?"

Scanlon reached wearily for another cigar. "It's all over for you two, but just starting for me. You don't think that nut's going to be an easy one to crack, do you?"

We were going down the courthouse steps when he came up, handcuffed to Mulholland's wrist. He seemed as erect and controlled as ever, but his eyes wavered and he turned away as we went past. I started to turn and look after him, but checked myself, and didn't.

It seemed strange to be on the street in daylight, with people around me. We went over and got in Barbara's car, and just sat there for a moment. She reached over, flipped open the door to the glove compartment, and wordlessly pulled out the bottle of whiskey. I nodded. She unscrewed the cap of the thermos bottle, poured it half full, and held it out.

"That's yours," I said, and took the bottle.

She sloshed the whiskey around in the cup. "Fine way to greet the brave new Sabbath."

"Isn't it? Look, there's no point in my even mentioning anything as futile as trying to thank you."

"Well, you could take me to Fuller's and buy me some breakfast. And give me Monday off; I'd like to send my nerves out and have them re-strung."

"Right. As soon as we have our drink. But I wonder if you'd answer a question for me? Why did you do it?"

She hesitated. Then the old cynical grin overran the tiredness on her face. "Well, it was Saturday night. And I'd seen the movie." She raised the cup. "Cheers."

We made it to a booth at the rear of Fuller's and ordered ham and eggs, and after awhile the crowd thinned out enough so we could talk.

"I'm sorry about throwing you that change-up pitch," she said. "I mean, over the phone, there in Roberts' apartment."

"What happened?" I asked.

"Well, the first idea didn't work out so well. I thought, in my simple girlish way, that if I just went to Scanlon and told him I knew where you were, I'd be in a bargaining position—that is, I'd tell him, if he'd promise to go along with this thing about Denman and the envelope. But it seems that when you have information as to the whereabouts of a dangerous criminal Scanlon's looking for, you don't sell it to him—you *give* it to him, or they run up and start sticking bars in front of your face. So I had to come up real fast with this old routine from the prison-break movies; if he'd let me call you, maybe I could talk you into giving up—think of the lives it would save. Actually, I'm not too sure he bought that either, but maybe by this time he was more than half convinced I could be right about Clement, so he agreed."

"What did you tell him to account for the fact you knew where I was? You didn't tell him we'd been together?"

"No, I said you'd called me from there to ask me some questions about Clement, because I used to work for him. You'd told me everything you suspected, and then after you'd hung up I'd decided the only thing to do was tell them where you were before somebody got hurt."

I looked at her admiringly, and shook my head. "All I can say is I'm glad you were on my side. But what gave you this idea of trying to bluff George with the envelope?"

"It was something you said. That he was too clever to leave anything to chance. The odds were, of course, that the envelope had gone into the New Orleans incinerator four or five days ago, but why settle for even a 100-to-1 probability when you could make it a certainty? And Denman could take the bribe without any risk, because there'd be no question as to his having destroyed the envelope; he just found he'd already thrown it away. The door was wide open."

I nodded. "You really baited it, all right. But I think the thing that finally broke his nerve was the wording. That indefinite deadline—the next half hour or so. He couldn't walk out right after you'd tossed this bomb on the table—that might look suspicious—so he had to sit there waiting for that phone to ring. Then, to top it all, it did ring. That did it. It was just Mrs. Scanlon, trying to get Scanlon to come home for breakfast."

She shook her head. "That was me."

"*What?*"

"It was part of it. As salesmen say, the clincher. I thought if he could just hear the phone once—"

I sighed. "Will you do me one more favor? If you ever decide to turn criminal, give me two or three hours' notice. I'll be out of the country."

She grinned. "You know, Scanlon said the same thing."

Scanlon was right; Clement didn't crack easily. They had to do it the hard way, with long hours of plodding police work, putting the case together bit by bit. They had to go all the way back to Florida, armed with photographs, and run down the Miami Beach hotel where the two of them had spent a week together when George met her while on that fishing trip. They sifted a mountain of checks and bank statements and other financial details to run down the money he'd given her to open the dress shop and the sums he'd been paying Roberts, through her. It was over three weeks before he broke.

Clement had searched Roberts' apartment, but he hadn't found the clippings either. They were in a safe-deposit box at the bank, and the key was in Roberts' wallet when he was killed. The wallet, of course, had been held in the Sheriff's office for Roberts' next of kin, so George was as much in the dark as I was as to where the clippings could be. They got a court order to open the box, and discovered close to $3000 in cash in addition to the news items his Los Angeles girlfriend had scissored from old newspapers, apparently in some library. The clippings contained her picture and the story of her disappearance after the Las Vegas episode. They never were certain what had made Roberts suspicious of her in the first place, but they did learn he'd been on the Coast himself at that time, October, 1958, on his vacation, just before he'd been suspended from the Houston police force. Probably he'd seen the story and the picture and remembered them—or at least, the picture. She was beautiful enough to stick in the mind.

It was Clement, of course, who'd tried to call her at the hotel in New Orleans the afternoon she checked out and came home. He had Denman's report, and was afraid she was going to be identified and picked up by the police before she could lose all her money and *have* to come home. He must have been scared blue.

It's been ten months now, and the memory of it is beginning to fade. Ernie took over the Sport Shop and is making a success of it. We threw out the furnishings of the apartment in the rear, and he's fitted it out as a first-class gunsmith's shop. Barbara is still out there in the office, but not for long. We're going to be married in January.

I sold the house and moved into an apartment, but about three months ago I bought a new building site, and a New Orleans architect is working on the plans now for the house. The lot—it's close to two acres—is up there on the brow of that hill overlooking the town just north of the city limits, the spot where Barbara and I parked that night—that long Saturday night neither of us will ever forget. It's a good location, with a fine view. Barbara agrees; she said I couldn't have made a better choice.

This afternoon we were in a back booth at Fuller's having coffee, with a tentative landscaping plan spread out on the table when Scanlon came in. He saw us and came back, and pulled a chair over to the end of the table. He ordered coffee too, took out a cigar, bit the end off it, and said thoughtfully, "You know, I always wanted to be a best man at a wedding, but somehow I never did make it. Now, unless you've got somebody else in mind—"

Barbara's eyes lighted up. "I think that'd be wonderful, don't you, Duke?"

"Sure," I said. "It's great."

"Well, that was easy." He struck a match, and held it in front of his cigar. "Here I was all prepared for a lot of maneuvering, and maybe having to bring a little pressure to bear."

"Pressure?" Barbara asked innocently.

"On the bride." He blew out the match, studied it for a moment, and dropped it in the ashtray. "I was just looking up the statute of limitations on a few minor peccadillos like harboring a fugitive, obstructing justice, and blackmailing a peace officer, not that I'd even dream of using anything like that if I didn't have to, you understand."

Barbara grinned. "No, of course not."

"Especially after the way you talked Duke into throwing down his guns and coming out of there that night. I'll always look back on that as one of the great inspirational moments of my career. I mean, when a peace officer can command that type of support and cooperation from the citizens, well, it gives you a warm feeling about the whole thing."

"Well," she said modestly, "I thought it was worth a try."

He nodded. "Yes, I gathered that."

He drank his coffee, and looked at the plan, which was almost unrecognizable now with penciled alterations. "What's all this?"

"The landscaping," I told him. "We've got it all just about settled except for this area here in back of the bedroom wing. I'm in favor of a swimming pool, with the rest of it in flagstone, but Barbara thinks the pool will be more trouble than it's worth, and that a simple expanse of lawn looks better anyway."

"I see." He looked at his watch, and stood up. "I've got to get back to work; you go ahead and thresh it out. But at least I've got an idea for the wedding present."

"What's that?" I asked.

"A lawn mower," he said.

OF SIMILAR INTEREST
AVAILABLE FROM OVERLOOK DUCKWORTH

DANCING AZTECS • 978-1-4683-0682-8 • $13.95

"Westlake knows precisely how to grab a reader,
draw him or her into the story and then slowly
tighten his grip until escape is impossible."
— *THE WASHINGTON POST BOOK WORLD*

OVERLOOK DUCKWORTH
New York • London
www.overlookpress.com
www.ducknet.co.uk

OF SIMILAR INTEREST
AVAILABLE FROM OVERLOOK DUCKWORTH

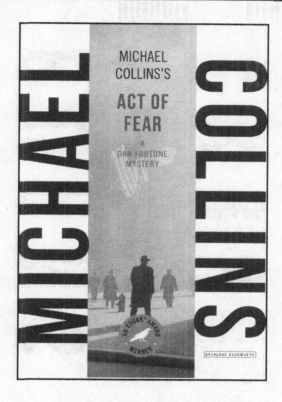

ACT OF FEAR • 978-1-4683-0726-9 • $13.95

"Collins is a skilled performer in the
Hammett-Chandler-MacDonald tradition."
— THE NEW YORK TIMES

OVERLOOK DUCKWORTH
New York • London
www.overlookpress.com
www.ducknet.co.uk

OF SIMILAR INTEREST
AVAILABLE FROM OVERLOOK DUCKWORTH

THE ALVAREZ JOURNAL • 978-1-4683-0727-6 • $13.95

"There is a toughness in this book, a hard-core, basalt
toughness, but also a leavening of human understanding."
—THE NEW YORKER

OVERLOOK DUCKWORTH
New York • London
www.overlookpress.com
www.ducknet.co.uk